Silent Chase

A Detective Ryan Chase Thriller, Volume 5

M K Farrar

Published by Warwick House Press, 2023.

This is a work of fiction. Similarities to real people, places, or events are entirely coincidental.

SILENT CHASE

First edition. February 5, 2023.

Copyright © 2023 M K Farrar.

Written by M K Farrar.

Cover art by Caroline Teagle Johnson

Chapter One

I wonder what Val is going to make for tea tonight?
That was the thought going through Tony's head as he increased the speed on the passenger train heading from Bristol towards Weston-super-Mare. It was always a slow chug out of the city, but the train soon picked up momentum.

Tony Iverson had worked this line for the past fifteen years. It was a long, straight track, and he thought he could do it blindfolded. If he was honest, it meant he wasn't always paying attention.

He reached for the insulated mug beside him and lifted the rim to his lips. As well as black coffee, the hit of the vodka mixed in with it burned down his throat. He'd have preferred a little whiskey rather than the vodka, but whiskey was too easy to smell on the breath. It was only a small drink, hardly anything at all, just enough to give him a bit of get up and go in the morning. He knew these trainlines so well, he told himself it didn't matter.

The passenger train containing several hundred commuters went all the way down to Penzance and back up to Paddington again. It stopped multiple times along the way, though most of the commuters had vanished by the time they reached Exeter and were replaced with families and students. During festival time, in the summer months, the carriages would be crammed with smelly teenagers who'd been drinking and living in tents for long weekends, and everyone would be complaining that there wasn't enough space on the trains.

It was no wonder he often felt like he needed a drink.

The smooth, slow clacking of the train was like a white noise that Tony found soothing. The countryside was beautiful around here, too, once he got out of the city, an endless patchwork of green fields stretching out either side of the rails.

He took another sip of his coffee and set it back down again.

Tony frowned and craned his neck forward.

Shit. Was something on the tracks up ahead?

He blinked a couple of times, wondering if he was seeing things. The object—whatever it was—was still at a distance. It was only a smudge against the metal, but, within seconds, the blur began to take shape. An animal, perhaps? A sheep that had wandered from one of the neighbouring fields onto the tracks?

Tony sounded the horn, giving a couple of short blasts, but already, in his gut, he knew it would do no good.

He'd had things on the rails before—it happened to most drivers at some point or another—but there was something about this one. He felt like someone had just doused the back of his neck with iced water.

Whatever was on the track wasn't going anywhere.

His heart hammered, adrenaline coursing through his veins. His head filled with visions of hitting it and the train derailing. He thought of all the passengers, how people would die and be seriously injured. He thought of the vodka in his coffee and how there would be an investigation and he would be the one to blame.

Tony hit the emergency brake.

The train was already travelling at seventy miles per hour. Since they'd only just left the city behind, it hadn't quite reached full speed. It was fast enough, though, and considering the size of the train, it would take time to come to a full stop.

Too much time.

He felt the change in momentum right away and knew the passengers would, too.

The thing up ahead became clear.

Oh God. That was no sheep. Now he was closer, it was plainly a person lying across the tracks.

A man.

He hit the horn, again and again, giving longer and longer blasts on it. Why wasn't the poor bastard moving?

He wanted to scream. Why were they lying there? Why didn't they get up and move away? Couldn't they hear the horn?

Though only moments had passed since he'd first spotted the man, the seconds seemed to elongate, stretching out like some warped bending of time. The colours of the countryside appeared too bright, the blue of the October sky almost garish against the horror that was about to occur.

They weren't going to stop soon enough. He knew that for a fact. The train was going to hit the person, and it wasn't going to be pretty. If the man was lucky, the impact of the train would kill him outright, but that wasn't how things normally played out. Committing suicide via being hit by a train wasn't fast. Most of the time, the person was pulled under the train, losing limbs, but the weight of the train acted like a tourniquet, a crush injury, keeping the person from bleeding out. Underneath the train was hot, too, and the combination of mangled flesh and hot metal was a smell no one should have to experience.

Tony braced his entire body, leaning back as though he thought doing so could somehow make the train stop sooner. Closer and closer, the train approached, until Tony was near enough to make out the man's features.

Oh God. What was wrong with his face?

Tony squeezed his eyes shut and swallowed hard against a rush of bile that rose up his throat.

The thud as the train made impact with the man was like nothing he'd ever heard before or wanted to hear again. It was loud, much louder than he'd ever anticipated, shuddering right through his bones to his core. And still the train didn't stop.

It felt like a whole lifetime had passed, when it was only a matter of seconds, until the train eventually came to a halt. It stopped harshly, most likely causing the passengers to hold on to their paper cups of teas and coffees to prevent them going flying.

Tony still had his eyes closed.

Don't look, don't look.

Would the windscreen be covered in blood and pieces of bone?

He had to call dispatch and tell them his position and that there had been an accident and that one person was most likely dead. They'd get the police here, too.

Keeping his face averted from the scene in front of him, he opened his eyes and reached for the intercom to make an announcement to the passengers. His voice shook, and was too high pitched, and sounded nothing like his own.

"I'm sorry to announce there has been an incident and this train will be delayed until further notice. I will update you as soon as possible, but in the meantime, if there are any doctors on board, can you make yourselves known to the train staff."

He doubted much could be done for the poor man, but he thought he might need a doctor himself. He didn't feel well at all. A sheen of sweat coated his forehead, and he trembled all over.

Tony let out a shuddery breath, then turned to his right, and vomited all over the floor.

Chapter Two

It was a bright autumn morning, and the huge train sitting motionless on the track appeared out of place in the serene countryside.

DI Ryan Chase pulled on gloves and protective outerwear and ducked beneath the outer cordon. All he'd been told on the phone was that there were suspicious circumstances surrounding a death on the tracks.

The British Transport Police had sealed off the area, though it wasn't easily accessible. A low fence ran either side of the track, separating it from the farmland. There weren't any roads directly adjacent to the rail track so the couple of ambulances and police vehicles had been forced to drive across the fields to get close enough. Though it was October, they'd been lucky to have had a dry spell recently, so at least the ground wasn't boggy.

The sergeant in charge of the scene caught sight of him and lifted his hand in acknowledgment. He said something to the uniformed officer he was standing beside and then made his way over to greet Ryan.

"DI Chase," the sergeant said. "I'm Sergeant Desmond Trotter with the BTP. I know we have jurisdiction here, but I believe this case is going to have a farther reach than just the train lines, which is why I hoped we'd be able to work together."

Ryan nodded. "I'll do whatever I can to help. Fill me in."

"We've got a male, Caucasian, between the ages of fifty-five and sixty-five, at a guess, hit by a train that had been travelling at high speed. The driver applied the emergency brake but, as is often the case, it was too late by the time he saw the man lying across the tracks. The driver is pretty cut up about it, understandably."

Ryan was still no clearer on what he was doing here. "So why have I been called in? It all sounds pretty cut and dried. Shouldn't this be a matter for the transport police?"

"Something happened to the victim before he ended up on the track. The driver saw something right before the train hit. He said there was something wrong with the victim's mouth. When we got a closer look, it was pretty clear what he meant. That was when we called you."

Ryan frowned. "How do you mean?"

Sergeant Trotter jerked his head towards the train. "You should probably come and see for yourself."

"Lead the way."

The stench of burning flesh and scorched metal filled the air as the two men walked towards the train.

"The train travelled a short distance after hitting the victim," the sergeant explained. "We'll need to walk down the track to reach the body."

Ryan followed the sergeant down the tracks, stooping down to get a view of where the body had ended up. SOCO had already been there before him, markers placed at intervals. Above him, curious faces were pressed to windows, trying to get a better view of what he was doing. Though the passengers hadn't been told exactly what had happened, they'd have a good idea by now. None of them were being allowed off the train. They were potential witnesses, and it would be better to keep them contained.

Sergeant Trotter came to a halt and dropped to a crouch.

The scene before them was enough to turn even the strongest of stomachs. High-speed train versus a human body was never going to be a fair fight. Blood spatter and pieces of flesh and bone coated the underneath of the train. Beside a numbered marker was a shoe, which Ryan realised also contained a foot.

Getting a post-mortem done under these circumstances wasn't going to be easy. It was going to take some time to put together all the pieces.

"It's the head you need to get a look at," Sergeant Trotter said. "I'm afraid it didn't stay attached to the body."

It was a horrible way to go, but hopefully it meant the victim had been killed instantly. People thought killing themselves via a train meant they would die quickly, but that wasn't the case. Too often, they suffered terrible, life-changing injuries, and survived, though perhaps wished they hadn't. Others simply took a very long time to die.

Ryan stared down at the victim's head, and the reason he'd been called in dawned on him.

The victim's lips were sewn shut with a thick black thread.

"Could he have done that to himself?" Ryan wondered out loud. "Maybe we're looking at someone with serious mental health issues."

Trotter shrugged. "That's what we're hoping you'll help us find out."

Ryan needed more details. "The driver said the victim was already lying across the tracks when he first saw him, right?"

"That's right."

"I think we need to consider whether the victim was there voluntarily or if someone else put him there."

Trotter arched an eyebrow. "You think this might be a murder? He wasn't tied up or anything. If someone else put him there, why didn't he try to run off?"

Ryan considered this. "Maybe he wasn't conscious."

"Or he was already dead when he was on the track?" the sergeant suggested.

"Did the driver mention seeing him move at all?"

Trotter shook his head. "Not that I'm aware of."

Ryan continued to examine the scene. He found the victim's torso, the arms still attached, though one was partially torn off. There weren't any marks around his wrists to indicate that the victim had been restrained in any way.

It was going to be impossible to know whether the victim was alive or dead when they'd been hit, at least until the post-mortem had been carried out. Would they even be able to tell if he'd been conscious at the time of the incident? They'd need to do a full analysis of the victim's blood to find out if there were any drugs in his system. But, from the extent of the injuries caused by the train, it would be very difficult to tell whether or not the victim had sustained injuries prior to being hit by the train. If the injuries were days or weeks old then perhaps the pathologist would be able to tell, but not if they were only a matter of minutes or even hours before. The body was so badly mangled, it was going to be hard work to get much information from it at all.

He sucked air in through his nostrils. "Are we any closer on finding out who he is?"

"Not yet," Trotter said. "We managed to get a fingerprint, which is saying something considering the state of the body, but he's not on our system. We haven't found any ID on the body yet either."

Ryan planted his hands on his hips and took in the countryside. "How did he get here? Which direction did he come from? He must have got here via a road, most likely the closest one. Are there any cars abandoned nearby?"

"I've got my officers combing the area," Trotter said. "If the victim did put himself on the track, I can't imagine he'd have walked far with his mouth like that without someone seeing him. We'll find a vehicle, if there's one to find."

Ryan glanced around again. They were surrounded by fields, all bordered with hedgerows. If someone else did put the man on the track, would they have hung around long enough to watch the train hit him?

How much time had passed between the train hitting the man and the first responders showing up? Would there have been enough time for someone to watch the victim get hit by a train and then flee the scene before any authorities showed up? Probably.

He didn't want to make any assumptions. Assumptions could easily lead an investigation down the wrong path.

"I'm going to need to speak to the driver of the train. He might be able to give us some idea about the state of the victim when the train was approaching."

Sergeant Trotter nodded over to one of the ambulances. "He's being treated for shock by the paramedics. There's vomit in the driver's cab, which he says is his. He's understandably shaken up."

Ryan experienced a twinge of guilt that he was going to make the driver go over what had happened again. He imagined the man would replay those final seconds over in his head in the days and weeks and even months to come.

"What's his name?" Ryan asked.

"Tony Iverson."

The arrival of Detective Sergeant Mallory Lawson caught Ryan's attention. She ducked under the outer cordon and jerked her chin in a nod as she approached.

"Morning, boss," she said. "What have we got?"

He filled her in on everything he'd learned so far. "We're just going to speak to the driver, find out what he knows."

"I'll take notes," she said.

The driver was sitting in the back of an ambulance, being attended to by paramedics. He was in his fifties, with a crop of thick white hair. His face was drained of colour, even his lips, and both hands shook as he clutched a paper cup of water between them and lifted it to take a sip.

"Mr Iverson," Ryan said, "I'm DI Chase, one of the detectives on the case. I need to ask you a few questions, if that's all right?"

He set the paper cup down beside him. "Yes, of course. And you can call me Tony."

"Thank you. What time did you start your shift?"

"Only a couple of hours ago. I left Paddington at six fifty-two this morning."

"Did anything unusual happen before now? Anything strange before you set off, or anything happen with the passengers?"

Tony shook his head. "No, not that I can think of. Why do you ask?"

"I'm just trying to figure out if someone chose your train in particular for this to happen to. I'm not saying they did, but it's best to rule out all possibilities."

"I understand, but nothing unusual happened." Tony shrugged. "It was just a normal day until..." He trailed off.

"How long have you been driving trains?" Ryan asked.

"Fifteen years now. I guess I'm lucky this hasn't happened to me already. I know a couple of drivers who've gone through it, and they've never been the same. One of them couldn't ever bring themselves to come back to work."

Ryan gave him a smile of sympathy. "I'm sorry you had to experience it. Do you know what time it was when you first saw the man on the track?"

"Just before half past eight. I called dispatch at eight-thirty, and that was only a matter of minutes after I'd hit him. I'd say I saw him at eight twenty-seven, and the impact was only seconds after."

"Did you see the man move at all?"

His forehead crumpled. "No, I don't think so. He was just lying there. I sounded the horn so many times, but he didn't even flinch."

"I don't know if you were able to tell or not, but were his eyes open or shut?"

Tony shook his head. "I don't know, I'm sorry. By the time I got close enough to be able to see in that much detail, I was completely distracted by his mouth. It looked...wrong." The driver shuddered and closed his eyes, as though that could dispel the graphic image.

Ryan had the feeling Tony would see the man's face imprinted upon the backs of his eyelids for many years to come.

"Did you see anyone else around? Anyone nearby before the incident?"

"No. It's just fields and sheep around here." He covered his face with his hands. "How could that man have done this to me? I would never want to kill someone, but now, here I am, a killer. He forced me to do it. How am I supposed to live with that?"

"We'll do our best to get you some support," Ryan said. "I imagine the train company will also have someone in place to help you through this."

Sadly, people jumping in front of trains wasn't an uncommon occurrence.

Tony threw up his hands. "No one is going to be able to do or say anything to change what's happened. No amount of talking is going to make a difference."

The driver let out a long exhale of a sigh, his breath hitting Ryan directly in the face. Ryan jerked back as a combination of coffee and alcohol hit him. Damnit. Ryan had been in this job long enough to recognise the smell of booze on someone's breath.

"Have you been drinking, Tony?"

The train driver blinked at him. "What?"

"When was the last time you had a drink?"

For the first time, colour filled Tony's cheeks. "Umm, last night." His gaze darted away.

"There's no point in lying to me, mate," Ryan said. "The breathalyser isn't going to lie."

"Yeah, okay. There's vodka in my coffee. It's just a splash, though. I didn't think it would do any harm."

Ryan had to stop himself letting out a sigh of his own. Things had just got even more complicated.

"Where's the booze?"

"In the thermal mug," Tony confessed, "next to my seat."

"I'll go," Mallory said.

Mallory climbed in the train cab and reappeared moments later, holding a thermal coffee mug.

She sniffed the top. "You might want to check this out."

Ryan took the mug and smelled it as well. The alcohol wasn't strong, but it was there. He got the attention of Sergeant Trotter.

"The driver has admitted to having vodka in his coffee. Has he been breath tested?"

Trotter's lips thinned. "I'm not sure, but I'll get it done." He motioned for one of his uniformed officers to breathalyse the driver.

They waited nearby while it was done.

"He's at point five," the uniformed officer announced. "The Rail Industry Standard limits for alcohol are twenty-nine milligrams of alcohol per one hundred millilitres of blood."

"I'll make sure he's arrested." Trotter folded his arms across his chest. "Obviously, the current driver won't be able to continue this route, so there's another driver on their way. They'll get the passengers to where they need to go."

"Do you think the alcohol could have contributed to this man's death?" Mallory asked.

"It certainly wouldn't have helped," Trotter said. "Maybe the driver would have seen the man sooner, or reacted faster, if he hadn't been drinking."

Ryan tutted. "He's going to have to live with this, and it won't help that he's been drinking. At least most train drivers, under these circumstances, can tell themselves it wasn't their fault and that there was nothing they could have done, but Tony Iverson isn't going to have that."

Mallory shook her head in dismay. "Imagine being forced to kill a person? There isn't really anything the driver can do if someone chooses to step out in front of a train. Don't these people consider that they might be ruining someone else's life at the same time?"

"I think they just see it as a big, inanimate object hurtling towards them." Sergeant Trotter glanced over at the train. "They probably don't even realise there's a person in charge of it."

Numerous faces peered out of the train windows at them. Experience told Ryan that most would be annoyed at the delay, rather than sympathetic towards the victim. If his gut was right, and the victim was either already dead or unconscious on the tracks before the train hit, then it meant they were each potential witnesses to a murder and would need to be interviewed. One of them may have seen something from the train. Someone standing in one of the fields watching events unravel or perhaps a vehicle cutting across the countryside as they made their escape.

Ryan addressed the sergeant. "I hate to say it, but we're going to need each of the passengers interviewed. Find out if any of them saw anything before the train hit."

Trotter grimaced. "That's going to cause one hell of a delay."

"It can't be helped. We're looking at a potential murder scene."

What else was around? Ryan made out the blocky shapes of a couple of farm buildings in the distance but not much else. Whoever chose this spot to put the victim on the tracks did so because they knew they wouldn't be overlooked.

Mallory offered him her thoughts. "If someone brought the victim here when he was already dead or unconscious, they would have had to carry him from a car or other vehicle."

"Good point," Ryan said. "How much does the victim weigh? He's not a small man. If he needed to be dragged across the field to reach the track, it would have taken some strength. Are there any drags marks near where the body was hit? Crushed grass or streaks in the mud?"

From past cases, Ryan knew not to immediately dismiss the female population as potentially being responsible for the crime. There was also a chance that it wasn't only one person responsible. If this was a gang-related crime, it could easily mean more than one person had physically put him on the track.

The track itself was surrounded by gravel. There was nothing obvious, but a quick sweep of a foot across it when the killer made his escape would mask any drag marks.

"We need to map out the nearest roads," he said. "Have we got any traffic cameras on them or any houses or shops with CCTV?"

Mallory twisted her lips. "I'm not sure. We need to get the rest of the team onto it."

Ryan agreed. They'd head back to the office and fill everyone else in on this new case.

"What are your thoughts when you see someone's mouth sewn up like this?" he asked her before they left.

"That it's a warning to someone to stay quiet."

Ryan nodded slowly. "My thoughts exactly."

Chapter Three

Mallory Lawson filed into the incident room with her colleagues, nodding her hellos at the members of their team already seated.

Ryan had got here before her and had already attached a number of printouts of photographs of the scene, plus a map of the location, to the board. Her gaze was drawn to the photograph of the victim's face and the black thread holding his lips together.

Who was responsible for doing that, and why?

The past few months had been hard on Mallory. After the attack in her home by Daniel Williamson, the man from Helping Hands who'd been offering her respite, she'd struggled. She'd managed to hide the attack from Ollie, her brother, which was a relief, but she hadn't felt safe in her own home ever since it had happened.

Daniel had been given a restraining order and told to stay away from her, but she wasn't sure she completely trusted it. It wasn't that she'd actually seen him anywhere, or that he'd tried to approach her, but she was plagued with the sensation that she was being watched. When she got home at night, especially when it was dark, she rushed to get through her front door, like a small child might run up the stairs after turning off a light, convinced someone was about to grab her.

She took a seat, but then their DCI, Mandy Hirst, appeared in the open doorway.

"Sergeant," she said, getting Mallory's attention. "You have a new constable joining the team today. Can you make sure he's shown the ropes? He's waiting in the office."

Mallory got to her feet to join the DCI. "Of course. Remind me of his name again?"

"DC Sunil Grewal. He's just finished his training."

Great. She didn't really want to have to babysit a new recruit. He'd have a mentor and a coach, but there was no better way to learn than getting your hands dirty, especially in their job. It used to be that people had to spend time as a police officer before getting into a detective role, but that wasn't the case anymore. Now they could get a degree and do work experience and use that to become a detective. She wasn't sure it made up for hands-on experience, but it wasn't her place to change how things worked.

The office had been filled with a strange atmosphere ever since they'd learned one of their detectives, DC Craig Penn, had been criminally involved in one of their cases. Their team felt like a family, and to have one of their own do something like that had left all of them unmoored. In their jobs, they needed to be able to trust each other.

Mallory followed DCI Hirst through the office to where the new recruit was waiting.

DC Sunil Grewal looked painfully young and completely out of place. He shifted awkwardly where he stood, and didn't meet her eye, even when she extended her hand towards him.

"DC Grewal, I'm Sergeant Mallory Lawson. Welcome to the team. Our DI is about to start a briefing, if you want to follow me."

He shook her hand, his grip limp. "Good to meet you."

She wondered how much he'd been told about what had happened to his predecessor, that he was now spending time in jail.

"You've joined at a good time." She tried to make him feel welcome, despite the bad handshake. "We've got an interesting case on our hands."

She led him into the incident room. "Boss, this is DC Sunil Grewal. He's joining our team today." She introduced the rest of the team. It still felt strange not including Craig's name. "That's DC Dev Patel, Shonda Dawson, and Linda Quinn. They've all been in the job some time now—"

"Some of us more than others," Linda called out resignedly.

Laughter rose around the room.

Mallory smiled. "If you have any questions, just ask. Take a seat."

He still hadn't said anything. Talk about a deer in the headlights. If he was this terrified just being around them, what the hell was he going to be like around actual criminals?

Mallory sat as well.

The rest of the office was a hubbub of noise—phones ringing, fingers tapping on keyboards, people talking. Ryan shut the door of the incident room, attempting to block out some of the racket.

"Ready to get started?" Ryan said, retaking his position at the front of the room. "Since Mallory already did the roll call, I'll jump straight in. As I'm sure you're all aware by now, a man in approximately his late fifties to early sixties was hit by the six fifty-two train leaving from Paddington. The incident happened on the track just outside of Bristol at eight twenty-seven this morning. We currently do not have an ID on the victim."

Mallory crossed her legs and set her notepad on her knee. Of course, she knew this information, but she listened, ready to speak up with detail that Ryan might miss.

"We have the added complication that the driver, Tony Iverson, had been drinking at the time of the incident. He was breathalysed to show he was at point five, over the Rail Industry Standard legal limit, and he admitted to having vodka in his coffee mug. Questions will be asked about whether he could have avoided the accident if he'd been sober, if he could have acted more quickly and stopped the train in time. The truth is, by the time drivers notice someone on the track, they're unlikely to be able to stop in time, but there's bound to be a media storm around it."

"He might not lose his driver's licence for it, though," Dev said. "I read about a train driver who was caught drinking a while ago, and though he lost his job, he was still allowed behind the wheel of a car. Doesn't seem right to me."

Mallory agreed. It should be a blanket ban if someone is irresponsible enough to get behind the wheel of any kind of vehicle while under the influence of alcohol.

Ryan carried on. "The train continued on the track for several seconds after hitting the victim, which made a mess of the body. As you can see from the photographs from the site, the victim was not only decapitated but also lost limbs as a result of being hit."

Mallory glanced over at the new recruit. He was a good shade paler than he'd been before they'd sat.

"The reason we've been involved in the case, rather than the British Transport Police dealing with it, is this." Ryan indicated a close-up of the man's face. "He was found with his lips sewn shut. Now, we don't yet know if he did this to himself or if someone else did. We also don't know if he was alive, dead, or unconscious when the train hit. The train driver said he was too distracted by the man's mouth to notice if his eyes were open or shut. We do know that the man didn't appear to be tied up or attached to the track in any way, so if someone did this to him, they most likely put him on the track either dead or already unconscious."

Linda put up her hand. "If he was already dead, why bother putting him on the track?"

Ryan nodded. "Good question. Maybe the killer wanted the body to be found? Maybe they wanted to create a scene, to get people talking about it? Make sure it got into the press."

"To get a message out to someone," Shonda suggested.

"Exactly," Ryan agreed. "The inference of the lips being sewn seems clear to me—keep your mouth shut. Someone is trying to keep something quiet."

"Could this be gang related then?" Mallory wondered.

"Possibly, though he doesn't exactly look like our usual gang suspects."

Mallory shifted in her seat. "He might be connected to them in some way. Working for them. Perhaps a job went wrong and he threatened to go to the police?"

Ryan nodded slowly. "That's definitely a route we need to consider. His prints weren't on the database, so if he is involved with gangs, he's been keeping his head down. Alternatively, he might have had mental health issues and just lay down on the tracks and waited for the train to come."

Mallory had seen the body, or what remained of it. She would never understand how someone could find it in themselves to end their lives in such a manner. It was so violent, so public, and it affected lives other than their own. Why choose to do it that way rather than a hot bath and a bottle of pills? Something more peaceful. Was it that they thought it would be more likely to result in death? If they'd done their research beforehand, they'd know that wasn't always the case.

Ryan took a couple of paces across the front of the room. "Until we've got some CCTV footage or had the results of the post-mortem, we have no way of knowing for sure. The train does have on-board surveillance, which includes CCTV in the driver's cab, so I'm hoping we'll have caught something helpful on camera. Right now, finding out the victim's identity needs to take priority. We need to speak with misper, find out if they're searching for anyone who matches our victim's description, or if any new reports come in that fit."

"How many missing persons in the system will match a white male of his approximate age?" DC Dev Patel asked. "There might be thousands."

Linda twisted to face her colleague. "Are we looking at someone who's recently gone missing, though? That's going to narrow things down."

Dev shrugged. "Are we? At this point, we have no idea. They could have been missing for months, for all we know, and it's only today that someone had decided to end their lives."

Mallory thought Dev had a point. Currently, they had no idea what the victim's background was.

"In which case, Dev," Ryan said, "since you're clearly already considering this from different angles, you can take misper cases."

Dev tapped his finger to his forehead in a mock salute.

Ryan nodded at one of his other constables. "Linda, can I put you onto the CCTV from the train cab? We should be receiving it shortly."

"Of course," the older woman replied, accepting the task.

"Shonda, can you convene with British Transport Police and find out if they got anything useful from the train passengers. They might have found some witnesses on board."

"Sure thing."

"DC Grewal," Ryan said, "welcome to the team. Can I get you to check into past cases, find out if we can link any gangs with the lips being sewn up. Has it been done before?"

"Yes, sir," the constable said.

Ryan arched his brow. "Call me boss or just plain old Ryan. It doesn't need to be sir."

"Yes—" Grewal caught himself. "Yes, boss."

Mallory found her boss's attention on her.

"Sergeant, can you check out vehicles from the nearby roads, see if we caught anything on ANPR or on any local CCTV."

She took her notebook off her lap and uncrossed her legs. "No problem."

She didn't know how far she'd get with that. The nearest roads were only country lanes, and even they weren't particularly close to the train track. The victim had got to the location somehow, however, whether he'd driven himself or someone else had. There hadn't been any reports of vehicles abandoned in the area—at least, not that they'd found so far—so there was the chance that someone had driven him there. Tracking down any vehicles that had been around the area at the time might not give them a direct answer, but it might uncover witnesses who would help them unravel the story surrounding the man on the tracks.

"Okay," Ryan said, "if everyone knows what they need to be doing, let's get started."

Chapter Four

Olwen Morgan reached for the glass of water on her father's bedside table and lifted it to his mouth. His lips trembled as he took a sip. She placed the glass back down and wiped the corners of his mouth with a tissue.

"Better, Dad?" she asked.

He nodded, but she wasn't completely sure that he understood what she'd said or that he'd even heard her. It was as though he lived in his own little world these days.

He'd started going downhill a couple of years ago when his wife, and Olwen's mother, Elanor, died suddenly after a short cancer battle. It was as though he simply didn't know how to function without her. Her death had left a void, not only in his life, but apparently in his mind, and things had only got worse as more time passed.

Olwen didn't know how much her mother had been covering for his memory loss while she'd been alive, and it had only become apparent to everyone once she was gone. The possibility left Olwen sick with guilt. How worried her mother must have been. On top of having cancer, which again she'd hidden, she'd also been dealing with her husband's vanishing memory.

Olwen didn't understand why her mother hadn't felt she could confide in her. It wasn't as though she was still a child. She was in her forties and didn't have any other responsibilities.

She'd never married, so it was unlikely there would ever be children on the cards for her. She pinched the rolls around her middle. No wonder no man ever looked at her in the right way.

That wasn't completely true. There had been a couple of men in the past, relationships she actually thought might be going somewhere, but they always left her in the end. They always said the same during the breakups, throwing similar insults. Who would ever want her when she looked like that? She'd never find anyone else. She'd been lucky to have them.

The worst part was she believed every word.

A light knock came at the door, and Olwen twisted towards it. "Come in."

The head of one of the care home nurses popped around the corner. "How are you getting on?"

"We're good, aren't we, Dad?"

The nurse, her name badge attached to the chest of her uniform reading Pippa, stepped fully into the room. "We're going to serve lunch shortly. Would you like to take it in your room, Mr Morgan? Or do you want to come out to the dayroom?"

Olwen saw her moment to get away, though she felt guilty about wanting to escape.

Her father didn't have many visitors. He was an only child. Olwen had an aunt, on her mother's side, but her aunt had never concealed her opinion of Olwen's father. Olwen's mother had already met her father by the time she was twenty-five, and they had her shortly after. Her dad was older than her mum by twelve years, so he was approaching forty then. Aunt Millicent must have seen him as an old man, and way too old for her sister, but they were in love.

She remembered being a teenager and her aunt coming around. Aunt Milly had done her best to put her feelings about Dad aside so she could still spend time with her sister and niece, but there was always friction between them. Olwen had felt bad for her mum, being stuck in the middle. It wasn't fair on her. She did her best to smooth things over, but her husband and sister were never going to be friends.

Her aunt was in her early sixties now but was one of those women who had refused to settle down. She had men in her life but never wanted to move in with them or have them move in with her. She'd often commented that men only ever wanted to live with a woman in order to replace their mother, and she had no intention of mothering anyone—including children. She'd remained happily childless, choosing to spend her money on foreign travel and property instead.

To any outsider, Milly probably sounded like the ultimate 'fun aunt', but she'd been as disinterested in Olwen as she had been any other child, and she'd been too busy living her own life to interact much with her niece. She'd grown even more distant after several fights she'd had with Mum, namely about Dad, and then Olwen's parents had decided to start up a foster home. Milly hadn't held back in telling them both exactly what she thought of the idea. It had pretty much been the straw that broke the camel's back, and Olwen could barely remember seeing her aunt after that.

Olwen pulled her attention from her absent family member. "I'm sure the dayroom would be better. It's not good to stay in here all day, is it, Dad?"

Her father's gaze shifted in her direction. "I'm not going out there if that arsehole, Bob, is sitting near me. I don't like that bastard."

Olwen and the nurse exchanged a glance. The particular man her father was talking about had died a month earlier, but no amount of telling him that made it sink in.

"Don't worry, Mr Morgan," Pippa said, moving to the back of his wheelchair. "Bob doesn't live here anymore, remember? He won't be at lunch."

"He'd better bloody not be. I'll show him my fist if he comes anywhere near me." He raised a shaky hand to demonstrate how he felt.

Olwen found herself pressing a smile between her lips. Her father was in no way capable of beating up anyone, even if the intention was there. He'd never suffered fools, had her dad, always making sure people knew exactly what he thought and not caring what their impression of him might be. She'd thought he might have softened with old age, that, with the Alzheimer's, might have come a more gentle nature, but that hadn't happened. He might not remember who she was most of the time, but he was still himself, deep down.

She rested her hand on his thin shoulder. "I'll see you soon, Dad, okay?"

There was no point in giving him a time or date. He wouldn't remember.

Chapter Five

Ryan took a sip of his cold coffee and set the mug down again. It was too close to the edge of the computer, so he had to pick it up and move it an inch to the right.

He scanned the rest of the desk, taking in the location of each item. Everything had to be in exactly the right place, or he wouldn't be able to focus on anything else. He nudged the pen pot to one side and then straightened the keyboard.

With a sigh, he sat back and dragged his hand through his hair, his thoughts on the case.

Was this even a murder? It wouldn't be the first time someone had thrown themselves in front of a train, though he had to admit them sewing their own lips together was unusual. The victim may have had ongoing psychological issues. He made a mental note to get Dev to ask around psychiatric wards if he didn't get anywhere with the misper cases, see if anyone recognised their John Doe as a patient.

The new recruit was sitting at his desk, positioned next to Linda Quinn's. As Ryan watched, the young constable picked up a pen, twiddled it in his fingers, before dropping the pen, trying to catch it again, and then knocking over a plastic cup of water he must have got from the dispenser.

Though Ryan had always felt DC Craig Penn had been a little too cocksure for his liking, he missed that confidence now.

Distracted, he checked his phone. Donna kept sending him listings of properties she was interested in. His heart sank a little more with each one. She'd already found a buyer for what had once been their family home. All she needed to do now was find a property she loved so she could move.

He struggled to pretend he was happy about the house being sold. Even though it didn't belong to him anymore, a part of him had always harboured the hope that he and Donna would finally put things behind them and she'd have let him move back in. He'd never stop thinking of the place as home, especially after all the time and money and love he'd put into the house and garden. It had been hard enough when he'd moved out and bought his poxy flat, but at least he'd still been able to picture Donna at home. To be able to picture their daughter, Hayley, there, too, even though she'd died.

Ryan forced his mind away from his personal life. He needed to focus on this case.

He wondered how the train driver was coping. While he would never condone someone drinking while behind the wheel of any kind of vehicle, the driver still didn't deserve to have been put in the position of being forced to take another person's life.

Linda called over from her desk, "Boss, I've gone through the on-board surveillance footage. I'm afraid it doesn't tell us much more than we already know."

He twisted his lips. "That's disappointing. Can you send it over? I'd like to take a look."

"I'll do it now."

Ryan pulled up the footage, aware it would give him the exact same view the driver had as he'd approached the body on the track. Would he be able to see if the victim was still alive when the train hit?

Initially, the view from the driver's cab could have been taken directly from a relaxation video on YouTube. On either side of the rails were the green fields of the countryside, and in the background came the clacking of the train on the tracks. If he didn't know what was coming, he could have sat back and let all his worries wash away. Instead, he checked the time on the footage and leaned forwards, linking his fingers together. His gaze was glued on the train tracks, watching for any variation ahead that indicated a body.

Ryan couldn't believe how fast it all happened. Between first spotting the body and the driver blasting the horn multiple times and hitting the emergency brake, only a matter of seconds passed. Though Ryan knew the driver had been drinking, he couldn't see how he could have reacted any quicker or differently than he had.

There was no time for him to have done anything else.

Ryan flinched as the train hit the body. Blood spatter hit the windscreen like a watermelon exploding. Just as he'd expected, several more seconds passed before the train came to a standstill. He pictured the scene beneath the train, the damage the combination of the wheels and the tracks had caused.

Though the driver would lose his job and be prosecuted, Ryan couldn't imagine him wanting to come back to it anyway. Like he'd said when Ryan interviewed him, he felt as though he'd been forced to become a killer.

Ryan had read up on interviews done with other train drivers who'd been put in the same position, and many said it had ruined them. Not only did they find it impossible to go back to jobs they had previously loved, it had affected all parts of their lives. Many were left with PTSD and were unable to work at all. They lost relationships and homes. Ryan bet the person in front of the train had never given a single moment of thought to the person in charge. All they saw was some faceless metal structure coming at them at full force.

It wasn't the easy way out.

Linda had been right when she'd said the CCTV footage hadn't shown them anything more than they already knew. He wondered if they were able to zoom in on the victim, would they be able to tell if his eyes were open or shut? Would they be able to see him moving?

He was just getting ready to watch it back over again when one of the other members of his team got his attention.

Shonda Dawson spoke up. "Boss, I've got one of the passengers saying they were filming out of the window right before the train hit the victim. I haven't had the chance to review it yet, but it might be worth seeing."

"Absolutely. Good work."

"They're emailing it right over," she said, "so it shouldn't be long."

"Let me know after you've viewed it."

Going through the tedious process of watching video footage might not be one of the most exciting parts of their jobs, but it was important. Cases had been prosecuted on the basis of CCTV footage—criminals being caught on camera.

Ryan took a moment to grab a coffee from the machine. Another detective wanted his opinion on something, so he got caught up in that long enough for him to finish his drink.

He attempted to return to his desk, but by then Shonda had already gone through the footage from the passenger.

"Boss, I watched the video footage," she said. "They caught something."

"Show me," Ryan said.

Shonda clicked her mouse a couple of times and brought up the screen with the footage. She hit 'play'.

The video had been taken by someone in the first-class carriage closest to the driver's cab. They were in their seat, filming out of the window. It meant they were pretty close to what had happened.

"I'm surprised they found a window clean enough to film out of," she joked.

Ryan chuckled. "It is first class."

Onscreen, the train passed fields dotted white with sheep. A small brook. A narrow country road, a white van driving down it, heading in the opposite direction to the train.

Ryan paused the video and pointed at the van. "See if we can get a number plate on that one. I'm not saying it's our mode of transport, but they might have seen something."

"Will do, boss."

A fraction of a second later, the train's horn blared.

Around the passenger filming, people murmured their reaction. The passenger continued to film, even when another horn sounded, and another in quick succession, then the brakes went on, and the murmurs rose in alarm.

The thud as the train hit the victim could even be felt in the passenger carriage.

"What happened?" Someone off camera shouted, "Did we just hit something?"

A different voice spoke up. "Let's hope it was one of the sheep on the track and not something else."

The person behind the phone camera swept away from the window to take in the confused, worried, and even irritated faces of their fellow commuters. The filming paused on them for a moment and then went back to the window. Over the tannoy, the driver announced that there had been an incident and that they'd be experiencing a delay, and also asked if there were any doctors on board.

Onscreen, they were back to looking at the side of the track and the small fence that separated the rail line from the fields.

There was movement in one of the fields.

"There." Shonda jabbed a finger at the screen. "That's what I wanted you to see. Is someone crouching near the bushes?"

Ryan leaned in closer. "You're right. Let's see it again."

She rewound it and replayed the footage. Sure enough, right after the point of impact, the camera caught someone half rising from beside a bush.

Frustratingly, the camera then swung away to film the reaction of their companion, and then the footage ended.

"If only they'd kept recording," Ryan said. "We might have seen whoever that was in the bushes get up and walk off. We'd know what direction they went in, and possibly even if they had a vehicle nearby."

She glanced over at him. "Do you think that might be the person responsible for putting the man on the track?"

"It's certainly a possibility. No one else has come forward to say they witnessed the incident happening, though they might have been up to something else that they don't want to get in trouble with the police for." Ryan thought for a moment. "Do we know if SOCO searched that area?"

"I'm not sure. I don't think the cordon stretched that far out. They focused their efforts around the tracks."

"Let's get them back there, retrace the route between the position the victim had been on the tracks and this area of the bushes. We might be able to get a print, or clothing fibres from the bush. If we're lucky, he'll have decided to have a cigarette or drink a can of Coke while he was waiting for the train and will have left his DNA or fingerprints there for us."

Shonda lifted her eyebrows. "You never know."

Criminals often did stupid things, even when they thought they were being smart.

Ryan watched the footage back again, this time, all his attention focused on the crop of bushes across the field from the train track. From this distance, he couldn't tell if they were male or female, but someone in digital would be able to blow up the image and clean it up enough to be able to see. It definitely seemed like someone was hiding there to watch. It made sense that they were the same person who was responsible for putting the victim on the track to die.

But why? What reason did they have for not only putting them on the track, but also sewing up his lips like that?

It was a question Ryan was determined to find the answer to.

IT WAS LATE AFTERNOON by the time Ryan returned to the place where the train had hit the man. In any other case, it most likely would have remained a crime scene, closed off to the public, but they couldn't close down a main part of a trainline for days on end.

The train was long gone, as were most of the emergency vehicles and teams. A couple of uniformed officers continued to man the cordon, and SOCO had spread their search area wider in hope of finding something that might be useful to the case.

A fence ran between the track and the fields, intended to keep wandering animals and people alike off the line. On both sides of the track, beyond the fences, fields stretched on.

Ryan had parked his car at the spot on the road closest to the line. He timed himself getting from the road to the track and then to the area of hedgerow where the video footage from the train had caught someone crouching. It had only taken him a matter of minutes, but then he hadn't been hauling a fully grown man with him, like the perpetrator would have.

He'd already sent SOCO to this area, to check for any additional evidence. They'd gathered a couple of items—a rusted can, a piece of plastic, and a few smaller objects, including clothing thread caught on a twig—but it was unclear yet if any of this was going to be any use to them. The items could easily have been blown into the hedgerow weeks or even months earlier.

Ryan squatted in the spot where the person had been caught on camera. He faced the train track. Sure enough, it gave him the perfect view of the area where the victim's body had lain. Had the killer got some kind of kick out of watching the collision happen? Or had they watched as a precautionary measure, perhaps worried the victim might make a run for it? Well, maybe not make a run for it, considering it didn't appear like he'd been able to move, but perhaps managed to roll himself off the track when he'd seen or heard the train coming?

He straightened again and dusted the front of his trousers off. Turning in a slow circle, he absorbed everything he could see and hear. There were only a smattering of buildings around this area, no road cameras or CCTV to have caught whatever vehicle the killer potentially used to transport the victim in.

It had been well planned, and this made Ryan suspect that the victim had been chosen deliberately. Spur-of-the-moment abductions and killings didn't play out this way.

Chapter Six

Mallory was pleased to be able to leave the office at a reasonable time, though it was already dark. The shorter days never used to bother her when she'd been younger, but she noticed them more these days.

She pulled her car up outside her house and turned off the engine. She stayed in her seat for a moment, as had become her habit, observing the street around her. Lights were on in the house, which meant her brother was home, as she'd expected him to be. She felt guilty about him being there alone, though she'd have hated to take away his independence because of her own fears. It still haunted her that he could have come home when Daniel had locked her in the cupboard. She'd told herself countless times that Daniel liked Ollie and wouldn't have done anything to hurt him, but then Daniel had acted as though he liked her, too, and look what had happened.

She checked her rearview mirror for any sign of anyone else. A car drove past, and she found herself shrinking into the back of the seat, as though trying to disappear. The driver of the car kept going, however, not paying her any attention. He probably didn't even know she was there.

Still, Mallory remained in her seat, her heart beating too fast.

She twisted to peer over her shoulder. On the other side of the street, a man walked with his head down and hands shoved in his pockets.

Her mouth ran dry. Was it him? For a moment, she couldn't even breathe, the air trapped in her lungs growing stale. But then she took in the man's smaller stature and realised it couldn't be Daniel.

She slumped forward, exhaling shakily. She covered her face with her hands. This was ridiculous. She couldn't keep doing this.

The truth was that she was still embarrassed. She'd made out to everyone she was fine, she was coping. She didn't want to appear weak in front of anyone—not her brother or parents, and certainly not her work colleagues. She'd always been the strong one, the tough one, the one who took care of everyone else. Now she struggled to sleep because she was constantly listening out for any signs someone might be breaking into their home, and she was too frightened to get out of her car in case someone attacked her between there and her front door.

She hated it.

Mallory let out another sigh and reached for the door handle. She couldn't sit out here all night. Her brother had special needs and was home alone, and he already spent too much time on his own as it was.

She opened the car door and climbed out, fighting against the panic pressing at her back that told her to run. Instead, she locked the door behind her and forced herself to walk at a sedate pace to her house.

Letting herself in, she called out, "Hi, Ollie, I'm home."

His voice came from upstairs. "Hi, Mallory!"

She waited at the bottom of the stairs, knowing he would appear at any moment. Sure enough, he stepped into view and then took the stairs down towards her.

"How was your day?" she asked.

"Good. I went down to the day centre, and Paul was there. We had fun."

Paul was one of Oliver's friends who also had Down's syndrome. They'd known each other for years now and were around the same age.

"Yeah? How is Paul?"

"He's good, too." Oliver pursed his lips, and his gaze darted to the floor. He twisted his hands in front of him.

She recognised the body language. "What is it, Ollie?"

"Mallory, don't be mad, but I want to move out."

"What?" He'd completely blindsided her.

Oliver spoke in his slightly stilted way, unable to say the letter R so they sounded more like 'W'. It was a young way of speaking, far younger than his true age.

"There's a house Paul lives in, and he says a room is free, and I could live there."

"A house? What kind of house?"

"It's a supported-living house, so we won't be on our own. He says they have lots of fun, and there is a common room where I can do my puzzles and other people can join in, too."

Mallory blinked. "Oh, right. Is that really what you'd want? It would mean you're not living here anymore. You understand that?"

His expression dropped, and she immediately felt bad.

"I've made you sad," he said.

"No, I'm not sad," she lied. "I just want to make sure you understand exactly what you're saying."

"It's just that you're not here very often, Mallory, and I get lonely sometimes."

"Mum and Dad come and see you practically every day, don't they?"

"Yes, but they don't live here. I'd have my friends at the house all the time."

She hadn't had anyone else in to help out after what had happened with Daniel. How could she trust another stranger in her home after going through that? She couldn't.

Their parents were getting older. She had to face the fact that they wouldn't be around forever. What would happen when they were no longer able to visit? Ollie would be alone even more then.

Was she just being selfish, trying to keep him here? She had always thought that she was doing it for his independence, but had she only been thinking about herself. Maybe she was the one who was frightened of being lonely. She didn't want to come back to an empty house.

The realisation hit her, and she swallowed hard against the constricting lump in her throat.

Oliver flung his arms around her waist and buried his head against her. "I'm sorry, Mallory. It's okay. I can stay here, with you."

"They're not sad tears," she said, forcing a smile and untangling him from her. "They're happy tears. I'm so pleased that you've found somewhere you want to be. You deserve to have company."

He frowned at her, his lips pursing. "I don't know if I believe you."

She placed her hands on his shoulders. "Believe me. Let me make some calls, and we'll see if we can arrange a visit to the house, see if you even like it there."

His goofy smile returned, and it gladdened her heart.

"Thanks, Mallory. You're the best big sister ever."

She lightly pinched his chin and returned the smile. "And don't you forget it."

Chapter Seven

The next morning, Ryan got to his desk early.

They hadn't made much progress overnight. They still didn't have an ID on their victim, but he was sure they'd get one soon. Most people had family or friends, or jobs they needed to go to, and when a person didn't show up at a certain place at a certain time, alarm bells rang. From the way the victim had been dressed, he hadn't looked to be a vagrant or someone who wouldn't be missed.

His team had been in touch with misper and asked that they let them know as soon as any reports came in that fitted the description of the train victim.

In the meantime, the pathologist, Nikki Francis, was conducting the post-mortem, and that would hopefully give them a few leads.

Ryan peered over his computer to where Mallory was sitting at her desk.

His sergeant seemed particularly quiet this morning. She hadn't been herself since the attack at her house. It was understandable. That bastard, Daniel, had knocked Mallory's confidence. Ryan couldn't imagine having to go home every day to the same spot the attack had taken place. Mallory clearly wasn't sleeping well—though she'd used makeup to try and hide the dark shadows beneath her eyes. He noticed it in her uncharacteristic slowness to pick up on pieces of information and the way she seemed distracted, as though her thoughts were always elsewhere. He'd suggested to her that she take some time off, but she insisted that she'd prefer to stay busy. He understood that. Hadn't he been exactly the same?

But this morning, Mallory was even more distracted.

He tried to get her attention, calling her name a couple of times, but when he got no response, he stood and went over to her desk.

"Everything all right?"

She looked up with that fake smile frozen on her face. "Yes, of course."

He raised his eyebrows. "Really? Because I just called your name, and you didn't hear me at all."

She closed her eyes briefly and then exhaled a breath of air through her nose. "Oliver wants to move out."

He hadn't been expecting that. "Really? Where's that come from?"

"He wants more company than I'm able to provide for him, and after what happened…well…it's not been easy for me to let strangers into the house."

"That's understandable. How are you feeling about it?"

"Mixed," she admitted. "I hate the idea of going back to an empty house, day after day, but he's right. He should be somewhere he can have fun and plenty of company. These assisted-living homes are hard to get into, and he already has a friend at the one where a room has come up. It's perfect for him."

Ryan folded his arms across his chest. "Well, that's great, isn't it?"

"Yes, it is. I'm just being selfish by wanting to keep him home with me. He's an adult, and of course he doesn't want to live with his big sister for the rest of his life. I want to do whatever is best for him."

"It'll give you more freedom, too." Ryan did his best to shine a positive light on things.

She snorted. "More freedom to work, you mean?"

"You could get back out there. Date?"

She rolled her eyes. "Oh God. Please don't give me dating advice. You know what happened with the last one."

"Not all men are like Daniel," he said.

"I know that, but you know what sort of situations we see in our line of work, so much violence against women. When you've been someone who's experienced it for themselves, it's hard not to want to protect yourself."

Ryan wanted to speak up for the male contingent of society but found he couldn't. It simply wasn't his place. Like Mallory, he'd seen enough violence against women to warrant her fears, and they'd even had one of their own involved in a case only a matter of months ago. No wonder she didn't know who to trust.

"Fair enough," he conceded, "but if you need someone to talk to about it, you know where I am."

"Thanks, boss."

The rest of the team had made it into the office now. Ryan spotted their new team member, already at his desk. Ryan hoped he was going to fit in okay with the rest of the team. Everyone had been more than welcoming, but the new recruit was still finding his feet.

Ryan called a quick briefing to ensure everyone had their actions for that day.

"Our priority has to be finding the victim's identity. Until that happens, it's going to be far harder to figure out exactly what happened to him."

"Are we still working on the theory that someone did this to him rather than he did it to himself?" Dev Patel asked.

"My gut is telling me this isn't suicide, but we still can't say that for sure. Until we know one way or the other, we need to keep our minds open. One thing that is bothering me is if someone else put him on the track, why didn't he attempt to move when he saw the train coming? He wasn't tied down, so he must have been unconscious or possibly even dead already."

"Or he wanted to die that way and lay there willingly," Dev said.

Ryan nodded. "We'll know more once we have the results from the post-mortem." He turned to Mallory. "How have we got on with any local CCTV or traffic cams?"

She screwed up her face. "Not great. It's a remote location. The nearest traffic cam we had was over a mile away on an A-road. With nothing else to go on, and no proof that they even used a vehicle, it'll be a needle in the haystack going through each vehicle caught on that road."

Ryan considered this for a moment. "I'm afraid you might need to search for that needle. See if any of the vehicles have been reported stolen or if any of the licence plates don't match the descriptions. Until we've got an ID on the victim, we're going to need to use whatever methods we can to investigate."

When the briefing was over, Ryan returned to his desk. He wasn't there long before his sergeant got his attention again.

"Boss, I just got a call from Nikki Francis down at the mortuary," Mallory said. "She's been working on our victim and wants to know if we'd like to go down there so she can run through her findings."

Ryan was instantly on his feet, grabbing his car keys from where they sat on his desk. "Absolutely. You coming?"

She grinned. "And miss out on the lovely aroma of a post-mortem? Not a chance."

Half an hour later, they'd parked outside the mortuary. They entered the building, signed in, and headed down to the basement where the examination room was located.

Nikki was already waiting outside the room.

"How are you both?" she asked as they approached.

"Oh, you know, same old, same old," Mallory said.

Something about her tone had Ryan shooting her a curious look. Was it really bothering her so much that Oliver finally wanted to be a little more independent? He'd have thought she'd have appreciated having the freedom. Or maybe it was that she was worried about living alone, especially after the attack. A familiar sense of rage rose inside him, and he clenched his fists. He saw himself as someone whose role it was to protect others, and he hated when arseholes like Daniel got away with barely a smack on the wrist when they'd deeply affected someone else's life. Though it wasn't the same, it always took him back to Hayley's death and that little prick who'd run her over and hadn't even stopped.

They paused to pull on protective outerwear over their clothes and shoes and then entered the mortuary.

Their victim lay on a metal slab. The train had made a mess of him, though Nikki had done her best to piece him back together. He still looked like something straight off Doctor Frankenstein's table, however. The post-mortem was partway responsible for that—the organs removed and weighed, his skull cut open and brain examined—but the damage caused by the train accounted for most of it.

The pathologist stood at the head of the table. All he could see of Nikki was her face and glasses, but it still struck him that she was an attractive woman.

Things had grown more comfortable between Ryan and Nikki Francis since he'd got back with Donna. It took the pressure off their interactions, though he was still embarrassed when he thought back to their complete disaster of a date.

At least he seemed to have got a handle on the OCD for the time being. He had no doubt it would flare up again if things got rocky, but he appreciated the easier times.

"Let's get started then, shall we?" she said, snapping on a pair of gloves. "Have you made any progress on finding out who he is?"

"Nope," Ryan said. "We're still investigating. Any information you can give us will be of help."

Nikki grimaced, as though she wasn't so sure of that. "I can only tell you what the victim has told me, and since this one didn't just have his lips sewn shut, he also had his tongue cut out, he's not been able to tell me much."

Ryan widened his eyes in surprise. "His tongue was cut out?"

"Yes. Cut with a smooth blade of some kind, possibly even a scalpel. I might be wrong, but I'd say whoever did this has had some kind of training. It's a clean job. Once the tongue had been cut, they cauterised it to prevent the victim from bleeding out. My guess is that they used the same blade they cut the tongue with, heating it up and then using the flat edge to seal the wound."

Ryan angled his head. "Someone who's had training? So, someone in the medical field then?"

"Possibly, though the work isn't good enough to be that of a surgeon or anything. The other thing that's making me lean towards that idea is the stitching of the lips. It isn't a rough job either. In fact, I'd say whoever did it not only has experience in working with skin, but also had the equipment to do it. The needle they used would have been curved and medium sized, designed for stitching skin."

"If they hadn't cauterised the tongue, and then they'd sewn his mouth up, would he have choked to death on his own blood?" Ryan asked.

She nodded. "Yes, most likely. They knew what they were doing. I also found formaldehyde on his skin, particularly around his face."

"Could the killer have used it to sterilise the equipment?"

"Quite possibly, but bear in mind that it's also used for other reasons. We use it here as a preservative. But it's also commonly used as an industrial fungicide and germicide, and it's used widely by various industries to manufacture building materials and household products, too."

Ryan pursed his lips, his mind running overtime. "That's helpful, thanks."

Mallory took a couple of steps around the table, studying the body. "It appears as though they wanted to keep him alive long enough to ensure he died in a very public way. But why? It feels personal, and it took some planning. Whoever did this is trying to say something."

"Kind of ironic that they're trying to say something while silencing someone else." Ryan addressed Nikki again. "Any idea how long before he was hit by the train that his tongue was removed?"

"Not long. I'd say a matter of hours. It hadn't had any time to heal, even with the cauterisation."

"Do you know if he was dead at the time of the incident?"

"From the blood spatter patterns and the volume of blood loss, I'd say he most likely wasn't."

Ryan pictured how it must have felt, lying on the track, mouth sewn shut, feeling the vibrations of the train approaching through the metal track.

"Unconscious then? He wasn't tied up, or even tied down to the track, so if he was conscious, he could have just got up and run away when he heard the train coming, assuming he wasn't there voluntarily. No one forced him to stay on the track."

"I tested his blood for drugs and found Rohypnol present. A large dosage at that."

"Rohypnol?" Mallory said. "The date rape drug?"

Nikki nodded. "That's right."

"But there's no sign of sexual assault?" Ryan checked.

"No. It's most likely been used to incapacitate the victim. It causes drowsiness and a loss of motor coordination, among a whole host of other side effects."

Ryan started to piece together what had happened in his mind. "In a high enough dose, would it allow a man to be placed on a train track and he'd be too out of it to know where he was and move himself?"

"Absolutely. I suspect he wasn't only given one dose either. He was most likely sedated for his tongue to have been cut out and his mouth stitched up. Repeated doses would have not only physically incapacitated the victim, it would also have affected his memory. He probably had no idea where he was or what was going on."

"That was probably a blessing," Mallory said.

"As for his other injuries," Nikki continued, "they're numerous. The train certainly did a job on him. The wheels decapitated him and partially severed his right arm and severed his foot. There are scorch marks to thirty percent of his body, where his skin made contact with the train wheels and track. He has countless bone breaks and fractures. I won't go through each of them now because we'll be here for days, but I've included them all on the report. The main contents of his stomach was his own blood. He must have swallowed a substantial amount before the tongue wound was cauterised."

Ryan blew out a breath. "Poor bastard."

He couldn't imagine how much pain the man must have been in, practically drowning on his own blood. First the cut of the tongue, then the cauterisation, and then his lips sewn together. What a horrific thing to go through.

"He hadn't eaten for some time before he was killed. There are the remnants of what once might have been a sandwich, but that's all."

"So, he'd potentially been held captive from the previous day?" Ryan asked.

"I'd say that's a possibility. Or else he simply wasn't hungry and so skipped dinner."

"From the girth of his belly, I'd say that's unlikely. He appears to be a man who enjoyed his food." Ryan considered something. "If he was being held somewhere before he was brought to the track, it means we have a second crime scene to look for."

"The same place his tongue was cut out and his mouth sewn up," Mallory said.

"Exactly. That sort of injury would cause a lot of blood loss. If we can find that location, we'll have a whole raft of new evidence."

She arched her brow. "Easier said than done."

"We follow the evidence we have. It'll lead us there, eventually. But first we need to find out his identity." He turned to Nikki. "Is there anything that'll help point to his ID? Any personal information that might help narrow things down? Tattoos or other distinguishing marks? Scars? Moles or birthmarks?"

The pathologist nodded. "There are a couple of things. He has a plate in his ankle from a break that happened a long time ago. I'd say a good ten years, possibly more."

Ryan wasn't sure how much use that would be. If it was a more recent injury, they could petition the orthopaedic surgeons at the local hospitals, see if anyone recognised him, but a ten-year-old injury made things a lot harder. The surgeons would have worked on a lot of people since then and may even have moved on themselves.

"Anything else?" he asked.

She went to the victim's head and opened his mouth. "He's recently had several dental implants. I can tell they're new because they were still healing at the time of death."

"Now that might be useful." He thought for a moment. "How many dentists do we have in the city?" he asked his sergeant.

Mallory shrugged. "I have no idea. Maybe twenty. Though I'm sure if you talked to anyone trying to find an NHS dentist, they'd probably say not enough."

"There's the dental hospital, too," Nikki said. "I think they cover people from as far down as Exeter, though, maybe even further."

Ryan considered the task ahead. "We're going to need to make contact with each of them. How recently do you think he had the work done?"

"No longer than a week ago."

"Good, that helps us narrow things down. The dentists will have records of the work they've done. Which teeth were replaced?"

"Top-right lateral incisor and the top-right canine," Nikki said.

"There can't be too many men who match his description who've had that exact work done in the past week. We just have to hope he had it done locally. If not, we'll need to expand the search. Until someone reports him missing, it's the best lead we've got."

Mallory nodded. "Agreed. We'll make it a priority."

Chapter Eight

Ryan got back to the office and made an announcement to his team.

"We have a potential lead on finding out the identity of our victim. I want all the dentists in the city and surrounding area divided up for us to make contact with them. We need to find out if they've had a man matching our John Doe's description in recently to have dental implants of the top-right lateral incisor and the top-right canine. If we can get a name, it's going to open up a whole world of information to us."

His team stirred with interest at this new piece of information.

Ryan wasn't done yet.

"We also know now that the victim had their tongue removed and cauterised before their mouth was sewn up, and they had a significant amount of Rohypnol in their system when they were killed. Considering this information, it's safe to say that we are now treating this as a murder investigation."

He let Mallory organise everyone to get all the dental surgeries covered. With any luck, they might have a name by the end of the day.

There was a second crime scene they hadn't yet located. Actually, two crime scenes. There was the place the victim had been abducted from, and the place where he'd been held and mutilated before being brought there.

Tracking down the victim's final movements would help narrow down the place he'd been taken from. If they could find that location, maybe they'd be able to get an ID on a car. But none of that could happen until they'd learned the victim's identity.

Ryan's phone rang, and he answered it. "DI Chase."

"It's Tim Bolton from forensics. I've uploaded the report from the train crime scene. I thought I'd see if you have any questions about what we've found."

Ryan sat back. "Thanks for calling. Did anything of interest come up?"

"It was all pretty standard other than a strand of something that didn't quite fit in. It's called woodwool. It's a product made of wood slivers cut from logs."

"Woodwool? What is that used for?"

"Any number of things, I'm afraid. Mostly, it's used as a packing material for things like hampers, but it's also found in stuffing for furniture like sofas. It's often used as bedding material for animals. It can also be in firelighters."

Ryan let out a breath. "Not much help to us then. It could have come from anywhere."

"It does come in different gradings," Tim said. "The strand we found is a medium grade, which still doesn't narrow down its use too much."

"Could it be connected to whoever was crouching by the bushes?" Ryan picked up a pen and twirled it around in his fingers.

"We've got no way of knowing. This stuff is found in a lot of places, and it's so lightweight, it could have just as easily blown from a nearby rabbit hutch as come from the person by the bushes."

"Okay, thanks, Tim. I appreciate the call."

"No problem."

The call ended, and Ryan placed his phone back down on his desk.

Across the office, his team were contacting local dentists, but it wasn't as easy as just placing a call and hoping for an instant answer. They'd be dealing with receptionists, who may not have immediate access to patients' data, or who might need to run details past multiple dentists who worked at their practice. Like most things in this job, it was going to be slow and tedious.

Ryan just hoped that by the end of it they'd have their victim's name.

Chapter Nine

Olwen left work late, as she normally did, and remembered she had nothing in her fridge for dinner. Her stomach felt hollow, but she really didn't have the energy to cook.

There was something depressing about cooking for only herself night after night, but she knew she couldn't live on takeaways her whole life. She was in her forties, and while she'd been able to get away with it in her twenties, she could see all those extra pizzas and chow meins sitting around her middle now.

She went to the local shop and grabbed a bottle of white wine and some stir-fry. She used the self-service checkout, though she hated the things, and put the items in a reusable cloth bag she always kept in her handbag. She tried to do what she could for the environment, though it never seemed like enough. No amount of recycled plastic from her bin would ever make a dent into the pollutants the big industries pumped into the air every year. Those were the sort of things that kept her awake at night. She didn't know why. It wasn't as though she was ever going to have children to worry about the world she was leaving to the next generation.

As she turned to leave, she collided with someone, and almost dropped her bag. "Shit!"

"Sorry!" a male voice said. "Sorry. Are you all right?"

She looked up to see who'd almost made her smash her purchases.

"Olwen?" the man said.

She stopped and blinked, the man's face coming into focus. She recognised him, but it took her a moment to place exactly where from. The last time she'd seen him he'd been so much younger—a teenager. He had an extra chin now, though she had a couple, and a lot more grey hair, though at least he *had* hair. Plenty of men were thinning or had already lost it by the time they were in their forties.

"Andy?" she sputtered.

"God, Olwen. I thought it was you. It's been…years. How have you been?"

"Good," she said, though her head was spinning. She felt like she'd just been picked up and transported back thirty years. "How about you?"

"Oh, you know. Not too bad. Well, actually, I'm recently divorced, but I'm getting through it."

"I'm so sorry." She wasn't, though, not really. She'd experienced a little thrill of delight at his news, glad she wasn't the only one whose life seemed to be a disaster. It wasn't a charitable thought, but she couldn't help it. Sometimes she felt like the loneliest person on the planet.

He flapped a hand. "Don't be. It's just one of those things. It didn't work out, but life moves on. What about you, Olwen? Are you married? Kids?"

Her cheeks flushed hot with shame. Why did people always ask those questions? It was as though you were a failure as a person if you hadn't met someone and procreated. What would she have done with children? She doubted she'd have made a good mother, and it wasn't as though the world was welcoming to new life. She could talk about poverty and war and global warming, but the truth of it was that, from her experience, people just tended to be horrible to each other. People were selfish and mean and cruel. She hadn't yet had an experience in her life that proved otherwise.

She'd always felt like her own parents had loved each other more than they'd loved her. They'd lived in their own world, and she'd only been privy to join when they allowed it. That didn't mean she hadn't loved them in return—she *had*—but it had always felt unrequited to a certain extent.

"No," she said. "Never really been my thing."

"Are you in touch with any of the others from the house?" he asked.

"God, no." The question surprised her. She hadn't even thought about them, never mind anything more. "I mean, it wasn't so easy to stay in contact with people back then as it is now. Everyone grew up and moved on and got on with their lives."

He gave a small smile. "Yes, I suppose they did."

"What about you?" she asked. "Did you stay in touch with anyone?"

"Yeah. You remember Tina? Tina Newton?"

Olwen nodded.

He continued, "Well, she's still around, and I still see Sammie, too. Samuel Cole?"

She fixed a smile. "Of course. I remember."

Olwen suddenly felt completely excluded. Why had they all stayed in touch but had never made an effort with her?

She remembered the girl she'd been back then. She'd never been one of the cool kids. She'd worn thick glasses and had a badly cut fringe. But in the group of outcasts, she'd felt at least partly accepted. Or she thought she'd been. Now, she wondered. If the others had remained in contact, but no one had bothered getting in touch with her, then maybe she hadn't been accepted in the way she'd believed.

They'd got up to some stupid shit back then. Sometimes she looked back and wondered how she hadn't ended up in more trouble. There had been the occasional brush with the police, but somehow she'd managed not to get herself arrested.

"We should swap numbers," he said. "It would be great to have a reunion sometime."

Her embarrassment deepened. "Yeah. I'd like that."

He hadn't mentioned her parents, and for that she was glad. She didn't want to explain her dad's dementia or how they'd lost her mum. She didn't want to hear platitudes and sympathies, especially when they both knew he wouldn't really mean it.

His expression brightened. "I'll put your number in my phone and then drop call it so you have mine."

She reeled off her number to him, and he did exactly what he'd said. She let the phone ring a couple of times before hitting the 'end' button.

Olwen waved the phone in the air. "Got it."

"Great."

They smiled awkwardly at each other. Should she lean in for a hug or a kiss? She didn't know what the protocol was for this kind of situation.

"Anyway," he said. "Better get off. I'll give you a text, though. Arrange something."

She nodded and then lifted her hand in a small wave. He returned the smile and then turned and left the shop.

Olwen exhaled a breath from between her lips and checked she had her shopping.

She'd take it home to microwave her meal and pour a very large glass of wine.

Chapter Ten

The next day, Mallory got into work later than she'd intended. Oliver was having a bad morning, and it only solidified her belief that him trying to live independently wasn't a good idea.

"Sorry, boss," she said when Ryan caught her eye.

"Rough morning?" he asked.

"Yep, and it's not even eight a.m. yet. Oliver didn't want to go into his shift at work, but I told him he needed to speak to his boss himself if he wasn't going to show up. He didn't want to do it, and you know how determined he can be. He ended up shouting at me and saying that he can't wait until he's not living with me anymore, and I shouted as well. I'm not proud of it. But how does he think he can live independently if he won't even speak to his boss himself?"

"Maybe he'll learn how to do those things if he doesn't always have his sister to fall back on."

She let out a long sigh and raked her fingers through her hair. She grimaced at the feel of the greasy strands. It needed washing, but there never seemed to be enough hours in the day.

"I don't know. I just can't see it happening."

"Just make sure you're not the one holding him back."

She sensed her defences rising. How could she be the one holding her brother back? She'd always pushed him into being as independent as possible. She loved to see him thrive. But had she been clingier since the attack? Had she been the one who'd needed him home rather than the other way around?

"I won't," she promised.

The new DC appeared beside her desk, managing to look simultaneously excited and nervous. "I've been calling around the dentists, as you asked, and I think I've found our man. One of the dentists called me back this morning with information on a patient, and it matches our John Doe."

"You have an ID?" Mallory asked.

He pushed a photograph taken from a driver's licence onto her desk. She recognised him instantly as being the same man from the train.

"His name is Gary Carter, fifty-six years old, married to forty-eight-year-old Julie Carter. We've got a recent address for him, too."

"Great work," Mallory said, and the new constable beamed. "Does he have any other history?"

"Nope. Six points on his licence for speeding, but that's all."

Not that Mallory was expecting anything. If he was in their system, his name would have come up when they'd fingerprinted him. Just because someone didn't have a criminal history didn't automatically mean they weren't a criminal. It just meant they'd never been caught.

"Did you hear that, boss," she said to Ryan. "We've got an ID, and an address."

"That's excellent." They'd still need to confirm the victim's identity with a DNA sample, but there didn't seem to be much doubt. Ryan got to his feet and addressed the rest of the team, informing them of the victim's name and other information.

"We need to work out his final movements. Where was his final proof of life? Dev, can you get his phone records, see if we can track where he went from those? What cell tower did the last call he made ping from?"

"Will do, boss," Dev Patel said.

Ryan directed his attention to Linda. "Can you request bank and credit card records? Where did he last use a cashpoint or his card? A shop or withdrew cash?"

"On it."

Mallory found herself under her boss's attention.

"How about you two go and see if you can interview the wife?" he said. "I've got to say that alarm bells are going off about the fact he's married but no one has reported him missing."

"This certainly isn't a typical 'wife murdering husband' situation," Mallory said.

"No, it isn't, but keep your mind open. It is suspicious that she hasn't reported anything. It's been days now. Even if he was away on a conference or something, most couples would have exchanged phone calls or text messages."

"Agreed. I'll find out where she was at the time of the incident."

"Do that, but remember she may even have an accomplice."

Mallory turned to DC Grewal. "Grab your coat, and we'll get out of here."

In the car on the way, she did her best to make small talk with the new constable. He was only twenty-six and still lived at home with his parents and grandfather—three generations under one roof. It was strange to think he was almost the same age as Ollie.

"They're happy I've a chosen career," he told Mallory, "but they'd have rather I went into medicine or even accountancy or law. They think working for the police is too dangerous, and they worry about me."

"That's understandable," she said. "My family felt the same way at first. What made you want to be a detective?"

He laughed, and it was the first time she'd heard the sound from him.

"You're going to roll your eyes at me, but it was all the television shows on the BBC. All those gripping crime dramas. I liked how the detectives were always in control."

"You know real life is nothing like television, right? We spend far more time behind our desks than we do chasing criminals."

"Yes, I know that now, but I'm still enjoying it. I want to be the good guy. The hero in someone else's story."

She found herself smiling. "Yes, I like that idea, too."

They pulled up at the address they had for Gary Carter. It was a modest terraced property. It didn't have its own driveway but had parking along the road outside. It was late enough in the morning that most people had left for work already, so they were able to grab a spot.

Mallory climbed out of the car and straightened her jacket. She spoke to the young constable over the roof of the vehicle.

"Remember that while we do need to question the victim's wife, there is also a good chance that she's currently unaware her husband is dead, and this news is going to come as a shock to her. We need to tread carefully around her grief but also watch and judge her reaction. Understand?"

"I understand."

"I'll lead the conversation. Just listen, take some notes, and then we'll talk about how things went afterwards, okay?"

Sitting in on the conversation would help teach him about breaking the news to relatives and following up with questions while also being sensitive about it.

Mallory slammed the car door shut, locked the vehicle, and approached the property. She rang the bell, then stepped back, almost standing on the new constable's toes.

"You don't need to stand quite so close," she said, looking at him over her shoulder.

"I didn't know you were going to step back." His dark eyes were wide.

"It's called personal space. You don't need to be in it."

"Sorry, sorry."

The front door opened, and she snapped back around, schooling her features into a passive expression.

"Mrs Carter?" she asked.

The woman was very tall and thin, with short blonde hair and the sort of mouth that suggested she'd smoked twenty cigarettes a day for a good portion of her life.

"Yeah, that's me. What's going on? Who are you?"

Mallory held up her ID for the woman to see. "I'm Detective Sergeant Lawson, and this is Detective Constable Grewal. We need to talk to you about your husband. I'm afraid there's been an incident. May we come inside?"

"My husband? You mean Gary?" Her features pinched. "He's not my husband anymore. Well, I guess he still is, but in name only. We're separated."

That explained why she hadn't reported him missing then. She hadn't known.

"I see," Mallory said. "I believe you're still his next of kin, though. We would really like a moment of your time to talk to you."

It wasn't only that Mallory needed to report the man's death to his next of kin, she also wanted to find out what his estranged wife knew of his final movements and his background.

Mrs Carter stepped back. "Guess you'd better come in then."

They filed past her into the narrow entrance hall.

"Can I get you a cup of tea or anything," she asked.

"Thank you, Mrs Carter," Mallory said with a smile. "That would be nice."

It helped to accept a drink when she needed to create a bond between herself and a member of the public. There was something very British about going through the motions of making tea. Upset? A cup of tea. Welcoming someone into your home? A cup of tea. Crisis? Cup of tea.

"And call me Julie, will you?" The word *you* sounded more like *ya*. "I can't stand all this Mrs Carter nonsense. I'll be going back to my maiden name just as soon as we get round to doing all the paperwork for a divorce. Costs a bleeding fortune, too."

"Of course." Mallory knew Julie wouldn't need to worry about the cost of a divorce any longer. She'd have a funeral she'd need to find money for instead.

Julie put the kettle on to boil and then set about dropping teabags into mugs.

"It was a fairly amicable separation," Julie said, chatting as she took the milk out of the fridge and a sugar bowl from the cupboard and set them down on the table. "We didn't have any kids, but he got the dog. I kept the cats. Seemed fair at the time, but I do miss that old boy."

She must have seen Mallory's forehead crumple at her sudden affectionate tone.

"The dog, that is. Not Gary."

"Oh, I see."

With the kettle boiled, she tipped water on top of the teabags and then handed them both a mug. "Probably best you make it how you like it."

They each added a dash of milk to the mugs, and Sunil dumped a couple of spoonfuls of sugar into his, and then looked guilty like he'd been caught doing something wrong.

"I like it sweet."

Mallory shook her head to indicate it didn't matter.

"So, what's this about Gary then?" Julie asked. "What's happened?

Mallory didn't give her a straight answer. "How about we take the tea into the living room so we can all sit down?

Concern passed across her face like a cloud. "Is he okay?"

Again, she didn't answer. "Let's go through, shall we?"

They followed Julie into the living room where they each took a seat around the coffee table.

Now Mallory got down to business. "I'm very sorry to inform you that a man matching your estranged husband's description was hit by a train two days ago and died at the scene. We do still need to confirm his identity via a DNA sample, but I've seen a photograph and believe it is Gary."

Mrs Carter blinked slowly once. "What? He's dead? How did that happen?"

"As I said, the victim was hit by a train."

"By accident? Or are you saying he threw himself in front of one on purpose? Gary was never suicidal."

"The circumstances surrounding his death are unclear, but we're currently treating this as a murder investigation."

"Murder? You're saying someone pushed him in front of a train?"

Mallory nodded. "Put him there, at least."

She covered her face with her hands. "My God. Is there any chance it isn't him?"

"Until we've done a DNA match, we can't say for sure, but like I said, I have seen a photograph of him and his body. Unless he has a twin, I'd say it's unlikely the victim is someone other than your husband."

"Why would anyone want to do that to him?"

"That's what we're trying to find out. When was the last time you saw Gary?"

"A few weeks ago, and even then, it was only by accident. We bumped into each other at the supermarket." She pushed her knuckles to her lips. "I can't believe that was the last time I'll ever speak to him. I wish I'd been a bit nicer."

"How did he seem then?" Mallory asked.

"Fine. Normal." She hesitated. "I mean, it was a bit awkward, as those situations tend to be, but that was all."

"Can you think of anyone who might have wanted to hurt Gary? Anyone he'd fallen out with?"

"He had the usual sort of fall-outs with people. Argued with the neighbours about parking spaces and people leaving their bins out when they shouldn't. Stupid things. But never anything serious."

"Did he mention being in any trouble? Money, drugs, that kind of thing?"

"No." She shook her head briskly as though to make her point. "Gary liked a drink, but he wasn't into anything like that."

"If you're separated," Mallory interjected, "how can you be so sure?"

Julie pursed her lips. "I've known him a long time. You know these kinds of things about people. I'd have picked up on it before now."

"What was the reason for your separation, if you don't mind me asking?"

Julie shrugged. "We'd just grown apart. People do. We were living more like friends than anything romantic. I guess I wanted more."

"You were the one to end things then?"

"Yes. He wanted to work at things, but there was too much resentment there. I couldn't keep trying to forget all the things he'd done and said."

Mallory frowned. "Resentment? I thought you said it was an amicable split?"

"Oh, well, as amicable as these things ever are."

Could his estranged wife have a reason for wanting him dead? Her mention of things he'd said made Mallory think of the victim's sewn-up mouth and cut-out tongue. What if this wasn't a warning to stay quiet but actually punishment for something they'd already said?

She made a mental note to look into Julie in more depth. Did she have any kind of history of violence? All too often, violence in the home came from the man and was directed towards the woman, but that didn't mean it didn't happen the other way around. Women could be violent towards their partners, too, but the male partners were too embarrassed and ashamed to seek help. However, it seemed unlikely that Julie Carter was the one responsible for his death.

Mallory picked up her cup of tea and took a sip. It was cool enough to drink now and not lose the inside of her mouth to scalding. She set the mug down again.

"I'm sorry, but I have to ask," she said. "Where were you the morning of the fifteenth, between seven a.m. and eight a.m.?"

Julie's jaw dropped. "You can't think I had anything to do with this?"

Mallory softened her tone. "They're just standard questions, Julie. I wouldn't be doing my job properly if I didn't ask them."

"Well, I was here. I leave for work just after eight."

"Can anyone confirm that?"

She thought for a moment. "Yes, my neighbour can. Florence, at number eight. She was leaving at the same time I was, and we stopped and chatted for a few minutes."

Mallory offered her a smile. "Thank you for that. It just helps us narrow down our investigation. Stops us wasting time following leads that don't go anywhere."

She blinked back tears. "I understand."

Mallory noticed that Mrs Carter didn't exactly seem overwhelmed with grief at the news of her estranged husband's death, but people dealt with grief in different ways.

She didn't want to upset her, but she still had to ask. "Can you think of any reason why someone might want to have kept your husband quiet?"

"What do you mean?"

"When we found the victim's body, we discovered his tongue had been cut out and his lips sewn together."

The colour drained from Julie's face. "What the fuck? Poor Gary. Who would do such a thing?"

"We're doing everything we can to find the culprit."

She was visibly shaken now, her hand trembling as she lifted her cup of tea to her lips, almost spilling it.

"Is there anyone you can call to come and sit with you?" Mallory asked.

"My sister. I'll call my sister."

They waited while Julie found her phone and made the call.

Her sister had clearly asked if she was okay as she replied, "No, not really. Gary's dead. He was murdered. Someone cut out his tongue and pushed him in front of a train." A tear slipped down her cheek. "Yes, yes, please. I'll see you soon." She ended the call. "She's on her way."

"That's good. You've had a shock. It's best that you're not alone."

Within ten minutes, Julie's sister had arrived. DC Grewal let her in, and the two women embraced.

Mallory asked the sister a few standard questions about Gary, and when she'd last seen him, and then left the two sisters to deal with their grief. She handed Julie her card.

"If you think of anything else, please do give me a call."

"I will, thanks, Detective."

Mallory thought of something. "Oh, one last thing. Obviously this isn't Gary's current address. Do you know where he's been living?"

"Yes, he has a flat in Hartcliffe."

"Do you have a spare key?" Mallory asked.

Julie nodded and then vanished into the kitchen and returned with a solitary door key on a chain. "Here you go."

"Do we have your permission to search it? It may contain evidence that will help us find who did this to him?

"Yes, of course." Julie's features were tight with grief. "Do whatever you can to find that bastard."

Chapter Eleven

Getting the identity of the victim had opened up numerous lines of investigation for them, just as Ryan had known it would.

Mallory and Sunil had returned with fresh information from the victim's estranged wife. The wife had no real motive, at least that they were aware of. They'd been separated a while, so it wasn't as though there was that moment of anger where a spouse might kill in an act of passion. Of course, they wouldn't rule her out completely, but Ryan wasn't going to waste too much more time investigating her.

Linda approached his desk.

"Bank records for the victim have come in," she said. "Looks like he used his card at five-fifteen a.m. in a corner shop just outside of Dundry the same morning he died. It was one of those twenty-four-hour garages with an independent shop attached, which was why it was open at that time."

"What was he doing out that way?"

"At an educated guess, I'd say he was on his way home from a shipping company where he's employed as a warehouse manager. He worked a night shift and finished at five that morning."

Finally, they had something solid to go on.

"Excellent. Let's get the CCTV footage from the shop and garage requested. It might be his final proof of life. We need to find out if he was alone and then track his movements after he'd left. Was someone already trailing him at this point? Where did he go after? If he was driving, his car must be somewhere."

Linda nodded. "Got it. One other thing. The address the bank has for him is different."

"That's right. Mallory has already spoken to his estranged wife. He moved out of the marital home six months earlier. We're getting a team to search the place so we can lift prints for a positive ID on the victim."

They had the permission from his next of kin, so they didn't need a warrant.

"You need any help with that?" she offered.

"You have plenty to get on with," he said, "but thanks."

Within an hour, Ryan drove to the flat with Mallory. With the flat potentially being a crime scene, he'd arranged to meet SOCO there as well as uniformed officers. They'd be able to tell if there were any blood spatters not visible to the naked eye. If the killer had used Gary Carter's flat as the place to mutilate him, they might have cleaned up after themselves.

Gary Carter lived in a two-bedroom flat in Hartcliffe. The building was a characterless red-brick block and was shared with at least twenty other flats. Gary's was on the third floor, so he had people living above, below, and beside him.

The arrival of the police drew attention from the other residents.

"We'll need to question his neighbours," Ryan said, jerking his chin at one of the other flats as a woman opened her front door to peer out into the shared corridor. "Find out what they know of him."

As Gary's estranged wife had a key to the place, it made their lives easier. It occurred to Ryan that Julie Carter wasn't lying when she said they had separated on agreeable terms. He couldn't have imagined giving Donna a key to his place when they'd first separated. There was no chance Donna would ever have given him a key to hers either.

Officers were already at the property, and Ryan took a moment to brief them on what they were looking for.

"We're searching for any signs that Gary Carter was abducted from this flat, so any signs of violence, blood spatter, or weapons. It's possible that Gary was not only abducted from here, but also that the mutilation to his mouth also occurred here. We need anything digital that might have recorded messages or emails, so laptops, phones, iPads, that kind of thing. Finally, we're looking for any signs that Gary made it back to his flat after the last proof of life we have of him at the corner shop. He purchased a Thai green curry, a two-litre bottle of milk, bread, and some eggs. His car hasn't been found anywhere nearby, but if we can get proof he came back here, it'll help us figure out the timeline of his final hours." Ryan clapped his hands together. "Let's do this."

The team worked slowly and methodically, ensuring every inch of the flat was covered.

At first glance, Ryan didn't believe this had been the location for either the mutilation or the abduction. The flat wasn't particularly tidy, but there was no sign of violence either. Nothing had been knocked over or broken, and as far as Ryan could tell, there was no blood anywhere. If the killer had used Gary's flat as a base in which to hold him captive long enough to have performed the surgical procedure of cutting out his tongue, there would have been blood everywhere. Possibly, the killer had protected the room with plastic sheeting, or something similar, which was then disposed of, but Ryan thought it was unlikely.

He went over to one of the walls and lightly tapped on it. Hollow. He stood still for a moment, listening. The voices of the upstairs neighbours arguing filtered down through the floor. To his right, the television from the next flat could be heard. If Gary Carter had been mutilated in this flat, Ryan was sure someone would have heard something.

"I found a laptop, boss," one of the officers called out.

Ryan went over to check. It was a big, heavy piece of equipment that looked like it needed updating, but it might contain useful information. If Gary's killer was known to him, they may have been exchanging emails or social media messages in the days and weeks leading up to his death. There was no sign of a phone.

One of the other officers called him into the kitchen. "I don't know if this is something of interest."

Unsure what they meant, Ryan joined the officer.

"Look," she said, holding one of the cupboard doors open.

The shelf was stacked with cans of dog food.

"Does he have a dog?" Ryan wondered out loud.

Ryan peered around as though he half expected one to come leaping through the kitchen door at him. There hadn't been any barking when they'd entered. A horrible thought occurred to him. What if no one had been here to feed the poor animal or—possibly more importantly—give it water? From experience, he knew the lack of water was more likely to kill an animal than a lack of food. But animals could be resourceful. He'd come across plenty of cases where pets had been found after a person's death, but they'd had the sense to drink water from the toilet and had, in some cases, decided their recently departed owners made for a decent meal.

This victim hadn't died inside the flat, however.

"His wife mentioned him getting the dog when they'd separated," Mallory said. "A male."

"Are there any signs of there being a dog here?" he called out to the rest of the team. "One may be hiding."

In his experience, it was cats that tended to hide rather than dogs, but that didn't mean it didn't happen.

"There's a lead on the coat hooks by the front door," another of the officers said. "But there's no dog here."

He exhaled a sigh of relief. Why was it sometimes easier to deal with dead people than dead pets?

Mallory frowned. "What happened to the dog then? Did the killer take the animal at the same time as the victim?"

"I can't think of a time I've ever known that to happen. Dogs tend to protect their owners, and a kidnapper wouldn't risk being bitten or worse by their victim's pet." He thought for a moment. "Can you contact his estranged wife, ask if she knew anything about what might have happened to the dog. Knock on some of the neighbours' doors, too. Ask about the pet but also find out if anyone saw or heard anything unusual recently. Did he have any visitors? Any loud noises coming from the flat? When was the last time they saw him?"

"Will do, boss."

Other than the laptop, there was very little of use in the flat. There was no sign of the food Gary Carter had bought, which at least made Ryan think that he'd been abducted before getting the chance to make it home.

Building up a timeline of the victim's final movements was useful. At some point between leaving the shop and heading home, someone had taken him. Ryan just needed to figure out where and when.

Chapter Twelve

Olwen didn't expect to hear from Andy, so when her phone buzzed with a text message just before she was due to leave work, she was shocked that he'd been true to his word and arranged a reunion.

Him: *Spoke to the others! They'd love to catch up, too. How does 7 p.m. at the Fox and Hound sound?*

The Fox and Hound. Just reading the name felt like someone knocking the wind out of her. It was the same place they used to get served when they were underage. They'd order wine coolers and Bacardi and Cokes, and feel grown up, sitting in the corner of the pub, smoking packets of Marlboro cigarettes. She had so many memories from that place, though she hadn't set foot in it in over twenty years.

Was she really considering going back?

Her finger hovered over the screen of her phone. Her hand trembled, her heart beating too fast, and, instead of replying, she tossed the phone back on her desk as though it had suddenly grown too hot.

She didn't want to look into all their faces and pretend like it didn't hurt that they'd all got on with their lives without her. She was torn between wanting so desperately to be accepted within a social group and her need to stay away and try to put all of that behind her. Hell, she thought it *was* behind her, as much as it ever could be.

Olwen made up her mind. She wasn't going to go. Maybe she should even delete his number from her phone.

The phone lay on the desk like something threatening, constantly catching her eye, drawing in her attention.

Would they meet without her? Would they talk about her? What would they say? She imagined Andy telling the others how fat she'd got, and how she'd never married or had kids. She wouldn't be there to defend herself, to explain to them that she had a successful career and people took her seriously and respected her now. She wasn't that same girl who'd hung out in their rooms, trying to act as though she was one of them.

Olwen managed to put the thought of the reunion to the back of her mind.

Work ran on later than normal. One of her accounting clients was applying for a mortgage and had decided at ten minutes to five that he needed to have the summary of his last three years accounts, and he needed them now. There was no convincing him that it could wait until the morning, and because she was conscientious and cared about her clients, she got him what he wanted. She told herself it was the reason she'd done well. Where other accountants might charge an extra fee for such a request and tell them it would take two weeks, she gave hers what they asked for.

Maybe it was because she wanted to be good at her job, but the other part of her was aware she was simply a people pleaser. She wanted to be liked, even by the people who employed her. Saying no would cause friction, and it was the sort of thing she'd turn over in her head at night, unable to sleep.

She made it home just after six, thoughts of the reunion back on her mind. Time ticked by. If she was going to go, then she'd have to get ready shortly.

She shook her head at herself. No, she wasn't going to go. She'd already made that decision. If she was happy with her choice, why was it bothering her so much? Why couldn't she bring herself to change into her pyjamas and pour a large glass of wine and settle down to an evening in front of the television? All of that was behind her now, and it wouldn't do any good bringing the past into her present.

Truthfully, it had been years since she'd given that time back in the nineties when she'd been growing up any thought at all. Her parents had closed down the foster home they'd run when she'd been sixteen and then moved to a different area. It had all happened so fast, she'd barely had the chance to register what was happening. She had a vague memory of being upset at the time, but she guessed that was normal considering she'd lived in that house her whole life.

Her memories from back then were patchy, only certain events standing out in more definition than others. That was hardly surprising. It had been thirty years ago. How many people remembered everything from their childhood? She certainly couldn't.

Olwen didn't have anyone she could share memories with. She was no longer in touch with most of her friends from when she was growing up. She'd stayed in contact with her childhood best friend, Helen, on and off, but they hadn't been close since they were in their late teens. Once they'd finished school, they'd just grown apart. Her mother was gone, and her father's memory had deserted him, so it wasn't as though she could share recollections with him either. Even her aunt refused to talk to her about their past. Maybe it would be nice to have someone to talk about the old times with.

She could just stay for one drink. Where would be the harm in that?

Her heart beat faster at the thought. She should do it. When did she ever take any risks?

Her mind made up, she quickly changed, let her hair down, dragging a brush through it, and applied a dash of mascara and lipstick. She wasn't out to impress anyone, but she also didn't want them taking one look at her and thinking about how she'd let herself go. She'd never really been comfortable in her own skin—not now and not back then either—but she liked to think she made an effort.

Twenty minutes later, she stood on the pavement outside the Fox and Hound. It was ridiculous how nervous she was. Who would be there? The whole gang? Not that she'd ever really been a part of it. She'd always been the outsider. Her hands shook, and she sucked in a breath. Her feet felt rooted to the pavement. The warm glow of the pub's lights slipped from the windows onto the road outside. Gentle laughter and chatter, the clink of glassware, and the low hum of music came from inside. It sounded welcoming, but still the thought of stepping through those doors and peering around for the others churned her stomach.

Come on, Olwen. You can do this.

She gave a curt nod to herself and got her feet moving. She pushed open the pub door and stepped inside.

She saw them straight away.

They were sitting at a round table in a similar spot to one they'd favoured when they'd been teens, drinks already in front of them. Olwen was thrown back in time, suddenly feeling like she was fifteen again.

She counted them—only three—one woman, two men. Olwen's shoulders dropped in relief, and she let out a breath. It wasn't everyone. She could handle a much smaller group.

Andy glanced in her direction, caught sight of her, and lifted his hand in a wave.

She smiled and headed over.

"Olwen," he said. "You didn't reply to my message. I wasn't sure you'd come."

"Sorry. I meant to, but work was crazy."

He motioned to the others. "You remember Tina and Samuel?"

Tina Newton and Samuel Cole. Yes, she remembered them.

Olwen smiled. "Of course. It's so good to see you again."

She studied their faces, taking them in. They'd all softened, it seemed, their faces no longer so angular, their bodies wider, their skin faintly lined.

We're middle-aged now, she thought. *No longer young.*

A wave of an emotion she couldn't quite place swept through her. Was it nostalgia for their youth? For time they could never get back. Or was it something closer to grief? She could never go back and live her time over again, and make different choices, take different pathways. She was in her forties now, and what had she achieved? All she had was her work, and while she took great satisfaction from it, it wasn't emotionally fulfilling. Her father probably only had a few more years in him, and it wasn't as though he knew who she was half the time anyway.

A flutter of panic danced in her chest at the thought of what her future held. She was going to be old and alone, and she couldn't see how she was going to change that. She was too old to start having children, and it wasn't as though she had anyone to have them with. Besides, having a child because you're afraid of being alone sounded like a terrible reason to procreate.

"What do you want to drink?" he asked, lightly touching the spot between her shoulders.

Her heart skipped at the contact. "Oh, that's okay. I can get it."

"Don't be daft. I invited you. The least I can do is buy you a drink."

Olwen gave him a smile. "I'll have a dry white wine. Thanks."

He nodded and went off the bar, leaving her with the others.

Tina stood to hug her briefly and then sat back down.

"You look exactly the same," Tina said.

"So do you," Olwen replied, though she didn't really mean it.

She remembered Tina with short spiky hair and a ring through her nose, not this almost mumsy woman in front of her.

She couldn't shift the awkwardness hanging around her. She hovered somewhere between not knowing what to say and worried she was going to start talking and not know when to stop.

"I can't believe it's been so many years," she said instead, smiling around at them. "What are you all up to now?"

"I've got two kids," Tina said. "Two girls. They're eleven and thirteen."

The news felt like a punch to her chest. "Wow, children. Congratulations."

"You don't have any yourself?"

"God, no. I don't think I'd have made a very good mother. Not enough patience for it, and I've been super busy with work, you know."

Tina wrapped her hands around her half pint of lager. "What do you do?"

"I'm an accountant." Even as the words left her lips, she found herself shrinking inside. It was all so dull, wasn't it? Her whole life.

"Great that you have a career, though. It's not like I even got my GCSEs. I've just been jumping from crap job to crap job, working behind bars, cleaning people's houses, that kind of thing."

"I've just been labouring," Samuel said, "though I don't know how much longer I'm going to do that for. The old body isn't what it once was. I swear I creak in the morning."

Tina laughed and elbowed him in the ribs. "Oh my God. We're not that old."

He arched his eyebrows. "My back says otherwise."

Andy came back with her glass of wine and set it on the table in front of her.

"Thanks." She took a large, nervous gulp, hoping the alcohol would go some way to loosening her up. "So you guys stayed in touch all these years then?"

"Not the whole time," Andy replied. "We went a few years where one or the other got tied up with life, and we lost touch for a while, but we always made contact again."

She wanted to ask why she'd never been included. No one had made any effort to track her down, but then she'd never tried either. Why was that? She hadn't even thought about it. She couldn't blame any of them for that. It was all on her.

"I'm sorry I didn't stay in touch with any of you," she said. "After we moved...well, I'm not sure why I didn't make the effort."

They all exchanged glances, and she suddenly felt like they knew something she didn't.

Tina offered her a smile. "It's okay, Olwen. We understand. We were all kind of thrown to the winds after the house was shut down. It was different for you."

Because she got to stay with her parents when they ended up in strangers' homes all over the city. She had stability—something they never knew. Had they resented her for that? She'd tried her hardest to be one of them, to be part of the gang, but she wasn't.

She never had been.

Everything about the foster home her parents had run had fascinated her back then.

Put a group of rebellious teenagers in front of a slightly gawky girl who'd never really felt like she'd fitted in anywhere, and it was like catnip to a kitten. She'd grown up in this sheltered home, with her doctor father and her sales-driven mother in her heels and business suits, with a couple of foreign holidays a year and her private school, then suddenly, she'd been introduced to a whole new landscape of society.

The property next door that her parents had purchased to start up the foster home had been almost identical to theirs, except a mirrored version, with three stories. A staircase with an old-fashioned wooden banister wound through each floor. The middle floor was for the boys, and the top floor for the girls. There was a strict rule that the boys were not allowed on the girls' level. Each floor had its own shared bathroom, and the ground floor was a shared kitchen and lounge which was referred to as a common room.

Where the Morgans' home had thick carpets with underlay and expensive sofas, the other house had the type of flooring more commonly found in office blocks. The furniture was all secondhand and bought for practicality purposes rather than comfort.

Each of the kids had a small budget for food, though Olwen was never quite sure if that was how it was supposed to work, or if her parents were supposed to be feeding them, including them in family meals instead of handing out money for them to take care of themselves. She remembered being shocked when one of the kids had showed her their food shop for the week—all cheap pizzas and chicken nuggets, and not a single vegetable in the bag.

There was no doubt that her parents saw both the house and the kids who lived there as an investment. They employed people who took care of things, so they never had to get their hands dirty themselves. One thing her parents had never been was nurturing.

Of course, they told her she wasn't allowed inside the other house and that she should stay away from the kids who lived there, but it was the nineties, and no parent knew where their child was or what they were doing back then. There were no mobile phones to track their movement or contact at a moment's notice.

The local neighbourhood hadn't been happy about the home being set up on their doorstep. It was the whole 'not in my backyard' attitude. Everyone agreed that these kids shouldn't be locked behind bars or end up on the streets, they just didn't really want them living on their street. Surely there were more...underprivileged...neighbourhoods they could go to? They'd never said as much to their faces, of course, but the gossipy whispers behind closed doors, together with the pursed lips and the disapproving shakes of heads said as much. These were the same people who would pat themselves on the back for donating to a charity or for baking cakes for the local school coffee morning. They didn't want to know about teenagers who'd come from violent homes or who had fallen in with the wrong crowds. They'd already made up their minds that they were troublemakers.

"How are your parents?" Samuel asked.

Olwen filled them in briefly, accepting words of condolences, before quickly moving on. She'd never kidded herself that her parents had been popular with the foster children—they'd all kept their distances from each other—and she preferred to talk about something else.

"Are you in touch with anyone else?" Olwen asked. "What about Wesley, or Anita, or Philip?"

The mood instantly darkened around the table.

Andy glanced down at his drink. "You didn't hear?"

She shook her head, her stomach dropping. She instantly knew it was bad news.

"No. What happened?

"Philip killed himself."

She clutched her hand to her chest. "Oh my God. No. That's terrible. When did it happen?"

"A long time ago."

She remembered the tall, skinny boy with his spikey black hair and dark eyes. He'd been the mischief-maker, the joker of the group. She remembered how the window of his bedroom had been directly above the front door, and he liked to throw water balloons out at whoever rang the bell. It was silly, playful stuff, completely at odds to the background he'd come from. She'd always warmed to him. He'd never acted hard, like so many of the others in the house had.

"Did you go to the funeral or anything?" she asked.

Andy shook his head. "No. I'm not even sure he had one. It wasn't as though he had anyone to hold one for him. I wouldn't have even known if I hadn't happened to be reading the local obituaries. I was on my break at work, and there were always newspapers lying around. I flicked through one and spotted his name."

"God, that's so sad. Why did he do it?"

They exchanged glances again, and once more, Olwen was filled with the sense that they knew something she didn't.

"Well, we all had our issues, I'm sure," Tina said. "We didn't exactly have the greatest of childhoods, did we?"

Olwen shifted uncomfortably. Her childhood had been fine. Happy...well...ish. She'd had a couple of rocky years where she'd lived next door to the foster home, and she'd got involved with them. But that was normal. Didn't most teenagers get into a bit of trouble and run around with the wrong crowd at that age? She'd pulled herself together once her parents had sold off the property and they'd moved house. Was that the reason they'd moved? Had her parents realised she was getting herself in trouble and so they'd made that decision for her sake? She couldn't remember there ever being any kind of altercation with her parents. One day they'd just announced that they were moving, and that was that. She did remember plenty of nights spent in the house next door, however. She remembered drinking cheap cider and smoking pot and laughing until her sides ached. She remembered being happy, but in a kind of tortured way. Why hadn't she fought her parents more to stay in touch with the others? Why had she accepted everything so easily?

"Come on, Tina," Andy said. "You know it was more than that."

Tina lifted her eyebrows. "We don't know for sure."

Samuel snorted. "Don't we? He told us what happened."

Olwen stared at them all in dismay. "What happened?"

They were looking at her like they couldn't understand why she didn't know what they were talking about.

"There were rumours, Olwen," Andy said. "Surely you remember?"

She felt like someone had punched her in the chest. "What? Rumours about what?"

"About things going on in the house that shouldn't be."

What was Andy suggesting? That Philip had killed himself because someone had been what? Abusing him?

A rush of heat hit her, and buzzing filled her ears. That couldn't be right. She'd have known. Someone would have said something.

She had to get out of there.

"I'm sorry, I have to go."

She stood, pushing her chair back hard enough that it fell over.

Blindly, she grabbed her handbag, then put her head down and headed for the door. Her thoughts swirled like a whirlwind, and she couldn't get enough air into her lungs. What were they talking about? No one was abused. Admittedly, it wasn't as though they were welcomed into the family, like one might expect of being in a foster home, but that could hardly be called abuse. They were just being taught how to be independent. After all, the moment they turned sixteen back then, they were expected to fend for themselves anyway. What was the point in mollycoddling them to send them into society and them not even know how to boil a kettle or put a washing machine on?

Clutching her handbag strap to her shoulder, she stormed out of the pub, moving as fast as she could without breaking into a run.

Going had been a mistake.

Chapter Thirteen

"I managed to speak to Julie Carter again," Mallory said, stopping by Ryan's desk with a fresh coffee.

It was still early morning, and he hadn't got much sleep, the details of the case turning over in his head. He'd managed a bacon sandwich and coffee for breakfast, hoping the salt, fat, and caffeine would rejuvenate him, but he was still shattered.

"And?" he asked.

"The dog died three months ago. She'd already said to me that she missed it, but I assumed that was because Gary had got the pet in the divorce and not because it was dead." She shook her head at herself. "To be honest, I'd completely forgotten she'd even mentioned it. Of course, if there had been a dog at the flat, and she'd known her husband had died, she'd have asked if she could go and collect it. I completely missed that."

"Don't worry," he said. "We all miss things. You've had a lot on your plate recently."

"Maybe, but I don't want it to make me bad at my job."

"You're not," he said firmly. "Don't be so hard on yourself. Did we get any more information from the neighbours?"

"Yes, though I don't know how helpful it will be. One of the neighbours saw him leave for work the evening before he was found dead, but that's all. There isn't any CCTV at the block of flats, either, for us to confirm the victim's movements."

Ryan exhaled through his nose. "Okay, so we know that he went to work that night, and then he stopped at the corner shop the following morning to pick up some food. It looks like he didn't make it home again, which means he was taken somewhere between leaving the corner shop and before reaching home."

"According to Nikki, there wasn't much in his stomach apart from his own blood when he was killed. If he went to the shop to buy some food, he didn't get the chance to eat it," she pointed out.

Ryan mused on this. "Does this mean he was taken shortly after leaving the corner shop then? Is there any news on tracing his car?"

Mallory shook her head. "No. It's as though it vanished with Gary."

"Damn. How are we getting on with the CCTV?"

"Not good. It's a rural area, so there isn't much to work with. Once he leaves the shop, it's as though he gets in his car and disappears. The footage from the shop doesn't show much either. He's the only one in there, other than the bloke behind the counter, and he says he didn't see anything unusual."

Everything was drawing a dead end.

"Have we got his phone records in yet?" Ryan asked, hoping for something.

"The final pings on his mobile are from a cell tower near where we have his final proof of life. Someone must have thrown the phone or destroyed it."

From somewhere in the office, a phone rang.

"We've got another one, boss," DC Shonda Dawson called over to Ryan, her expression concerned. "Another victim with their mouth sewn shut and then killed. This one has been thrown from the top of a bridge, right in front of an HGV. The driver's pretty shaken up, understandably."

The familiar burst of adrenaline shot through his veins.

"Let's get out there." He informed the rest of his team of the incident. "You want to drive with me, Mallory?" he asked his sergeant.

She gave a curt nod. "Absolutely."

It took them longer than he would have liked to get across the city. It was rush-hour traffic, which was always a nightmare in Bristol, but now made a hundred times worse by the incident.

Commuters were being diverted, but there was already a long tailback in both directions. In the distance came the blast of horns, drivers giving voice to their irritation in the only way they knew how. Ryan shook his head at them, though they couldn't see him. He didn't know why people thought leaning on their horns would make the slightest bit of difference. The road was closed because someone had been murdered, and they weren't going to reopen it just because they made some noise.

It took them some time to weave through all the traffic that had come to a standstill and was now building up behind them. Some drivers, thinking they were being useful, had pulled onto the hard shoulder, so all they'd achieved was blocking more of the road up. Idiots. Then other drivers had driven into their empty spaces, so even when they had police and ambulances up behind them, with sirens and lights going, they had nowhere they could pull back into. Though it was Ryan's job to protect the general public, there were some of them who needed their heads bashing together.

"This is madness." Mallory shook her head.

"Multiple vehicles were involved," he said, "and we're not even here about that side of things. We'll leave that up to the traffic police. It's our job to focus on the victim."

They finally got through the traffic, and Ryan stopped the car.

The traffic police were already at the scene, the road closed both ways. The area was a hive of activity. Though the lorry had been the one to hit the victim, the sudden stop had caused a pileup. Several cars had gone into the backs of each other when the driver of the lorry had slammed on the brakes to try and avoid the victim. Special Forensic Collision Investigators would be brought in, who would examine the scene and vehicles involved and make sure all the evidence was recorded. They'd then produce a reconstruction report which would help to explain exactly how the crash had unfolded.

Ryan hoped no one else had been killed as a result.

Multiple ambulances had already arrived for the victim and those injured during the crash. Above, an air ambulance hovered, searching for a nearby field that would be convenient to set down in.

They climbed out, putting on protective gloves as they did so.

A uniformed police officer signed them in, and they ducked under the cordon tape and walked towards the position of the body. A privacy tent had already been erected around it.

The sergeant in charge of the scene approached them. She appeared harried, though that was hardly surprising, given the magnitude of the incident.

"Detectives, I'm Sergeant Louise Short. Thank you for coming. As you can see, this is an absolute mess."

"I hope no one else has been killed or too badly hurt," Mallory said, glancing back at the ambulances and crumpled cars.

"No fatal casualties, as of yet," she said. "Not including the original victim, of course. The victim is female, in her fifties or sixties, at a guess."

Ryan wasn't sure why, but he hadn't been expecting the victim to be female. He'd been hoping there wouldn't be a second victim at all, and the first had been a one-off, but that clearly wasn't the case.

"Do we know who she is?" Mallory asked.

Sergeant Short shook her head. "Not yet. No sign of any ID on the body, and her prints aren't in the system."

Ryan glanced up at the overhead footbridge that ran from one side of the A-road to the other. It was an industrial structure of concrete and metal.

"Was that where the victim jumped, or was most likely pushed from?"

Short followed his line of sight. "That's right. We've closed the bridge off from both ends, too, and I've been up there to search for any evidence myself. Thought she might have left a handbag up there or something, but there's no sign of anything."

"I don't believe she's a jumper," Ryan said. "I highly doubt she'd have had her handbag with her."

"No, but we were unaware of your previous case at that point. You think the two cases are connected?"

"With the sewn mouths? Yes, I'd say it's a near certainty. She didn't do this to herself, so unless we have a copycat killer, I believe the same person is responsible. Let's take a look at the victim, shall we?"

"This way."

Sergeant Short led them over to where the privacy tent shielded the body. With this being a murder enquiry, they hadn't wanted to move her, and with all the other victims from the pileup around, erecting a tent had been the most sensible choice.

Ryan followed the police sergeant inside, with Mallory close behind. The victim wasn't in quite such a bad state as the one who'd been hit by the train, but she wasn't far off.

Both the impact of the fall, and the impact of the front of the lorry, had produced devastating results. From the angle of her limbs, it was clear she had multiple broken bones. The side of her skull was partially caved in, and her face was bloodied and battered.

He dropped to a crouch and inspected the black thread that had been used to sew up her lips. He was no expert in that field, but it looked to him to be exactly the same as the thread that was used on the first victim. Forensics would be able to compare the two threads and know if they came from the same reel. Had this woman also had her tongue removed? There was a lot of blood, but it was impossible to know whether that had been caused in the accident or if she was already bloodied when she was pushed.

"Is it the same MO?" the sergeant asked.

"We'll know more after the post-mortem, but it certainly looks the same." He glanced over his shoulder. "Would you agree, DS Lawson?"

Mallory nodded. "Yes, it does. And while they used a lorry instead of a train to actually kill the victim, we can't ignore the similarities of them being hit by a large vehicle at a high speed."

He hoped the victim had at least been killed instantly upon impact—that's if she wasn't already dead before she'd fallen. If, like with the previous victim, she was also doped up, there was a good chance she wouldn't have been completely aware of what was happening.

Ryan scanned the woman's body for any clues to her identity. Her hair was dyed a dark brown, thinning at the scalp where the grey was growing through. Mascara was smudged beneath her eyes. Her eyebrows had been shaped and filled in. Her clothes were smart—a blood-soaked chiffon scarf with butterflies on it still wrapped around her neck. She appeared to be the sort of woman who took care of herself.

"Check out her hands," he said. The middle fingers of both were heavy with jewellery. Mostly gold rings, with huge stones in various shapes, sizes, and settings. "Whoever did this didn't attempt to steal from her."

"Certainly doesn't look that way," Mallory agreed. "But then we never really thought these were theft-motivated killings."

"I don't think we're going to have too much difficulty in IDing her. Someone is going to be missing her pretty soon. I just wish we were able to give her family better news."

They stepped out of the privacy tent.

"What other details do you have?" Ryan asked Sergeant Short.

"The incident happened at approximately eight-oh-five this morning. We have a number of witnesses, including the driver of the lorry. Traffic was busy, as it was rush hour, so we've got drivers of the cars directly behind him as well. We'll have to do a callout for those who were ahead to see if we can get people to come forward. They might have seen something as well."

"Any traffic cameras around?"

She shook his head. "Not on this bridge. I'm guessing whoever threw her over did their research."

"We need to talk to the driver of the lorry," Ryan said. "Where is he?"

"In the back of one of the ambulances. His name's Freddie Adams. The airbag went off when the accident happened, and he's got a bloodied nose and some bruising. The seatbelt may have fractured one of his ribs, so the paramedics want to take him in for observation. I managed to hold them off until you'd had the chance to speak to him. He's not in any danger."

"Thank you."

The driver of the lorry was a man in his thirties. He sat in the back of the ambulance with a neck brace on. His hands trembled as he knotted them in his hair.

"Freddie Adams?" Ryan asked.

The man glanced up and nodded. He had dark bruises under his eyes, the bridge of his nose was swollen, and red friction marks crisscrossed his jaw where the airbag had hit.

"I'm DI Chase, and this is DS Lawson. We'd like to ask you some questions about what happened today, if you're feeling up to it."

"Yes, I'm okay. Unlike that poor woman. She's dead, isn't she?"

"I'm afraid so."

He closed his eyes briefly. "I knew no one could survive that. As if the fall wouldn't have been bad enough, to also have the front of my lorry hit her...God."

"Can you tell me what happened before the accident? Where are you driving from and to?"

"I was coming from a depot in Somerset. Left about five a.m. and got to my destination around six-thirty. We unloaded, and I got on the road again. I'd only been driving about twenty minutes when this happened."

"When you were approaching the footbridge, what did you see first?"

"There were definitely two people standing up there. I often look up when I'm about to go under a bridge. Not so much for jumpers or anything, but sometimes you get kids who want you to blow your horn, and other times you get little assholes who throw stones down onto the windscreen. It's just become habitual now, you know. I glanced up and saw two figures there, but I didn't really think anything of it. They must have crossed to the other side of the bridge, and just as I passed under it, one of the people dropped down right in front of me." He shuddered. "I'll never forget that sound," he said, "the bang when her body hit the front of the lorry. It's going to fucking haunt me."

"Did you notice if the victim was pushed or thrown, or if she jumped?"

He shook his head, slowly. "I couldn't tell you, mate, sorry. They were standing side by side, and then the woman flew through the air right in front of me, and I hit her. There was nothing I could do. It all happened so fast. I slammed on my brakes, but of course there were other vehicles all around me. A car went into the back of me, and because I'd automatically swerved to try to avoid the woman, I took out the car beside me, too. Are they all right? The people in the cars, I mean. I'll never forgive myself if I killed someone else, too."

"It wasn't your fault," Ryan reassured him. "And we have paramedics taking care of everyone. Don't worry about them. Have you been checked over yourself?"

"Yeah. I'm all right."

Nearby, someone cleared their throat in disagreement.

"We really need to take him into hospital," one of the paramedics interrupted, "just as soon as you're done. You need to be properly checked over, Mr Adams."

"I'm okay, just a bit bruised from the airbag and seatbelt."

"You have a possible broken nose and fractured ribs. You need to be in hospital." The paramedic sent Ryan a disapproving glare for keeping the driver out of hospital for so long.

"I think you should listen to the professionals," Ryan said. "If we need to speak to you in more detail, we can come to the hospital."

"Sure, thanks."

One of the uniformed officers had already taken the man's details down, so they could get in touch with him again, even if he was discharged quickly.

Ryan and Mallory stepped away from the ambulance so they were out of earshot.

"If the driver noticed two people on the bridge," Mallory said, "then there's a good chance others did, too. We might even be able to get a description of the killer from someone."

"We could certainly do with a decent lead," he agreed.

Mallory glanced back towards the other vehicles. "I'm going to see how uniform are getting on with questioning any other witnesses."

"Thanks. I'll take a look up on the bridge, see if there's anything there that'll be of help to us."

Technically, though the victim had been killed on the road, the bridge itself was the main crime scene, other than the location where she had her lips sewn together. It was the place where the killer had thrown the victim from.

To reach the bridge, Ryan had to leave the main road. He swung his leg over the top of the concrete barrier dividing the lanes from the grassy verge beyond, and then crossed it to where he ended up on another, much smaller road. He took a left and walked towards the start of the bridge.

The bridge had also been closed from both sides, blue police tape fluttering in the breeze. On both ends, the bridge wound back on itself, before straightening out as it led over the top of the road.

Ryan stopped at the bottom and took in his surroundings. It was a residential area; the occupants of the houses must not have minded being so close to the motorway, unless they'd bought the properties before the motorway had been built. He imagined the uproar that must have caused. No one wanted a main road to run behind their back garden.

Did any of these homes have CCTV? He'd make sure they went door to door, asking if anyone was home at the time of the incident and if they saw anything. Would the killer have scoped out this area beforehand? The way this all seemed to have been planned out, Ryan thought that they would have. If so, they needed to ask the local residents if they'd seen someone suspicious hanging around over the previous days or possibly even weeks.

What about transport? How was the killer getting their victim to and from the place where they were killed? While they might have been on foot, certainly at least over the bridge, Ryan doubted they'd have been travelling that way the whole time. It meant the killer had a car, and cars could be traced. How long had they been standing on the bridge before the victim was thrown? If they could narrow down that time, then they could look at any vehicles caught on local traffic cameras.

One thing they didn't yet have was the identity of the woman. Just like with the first victim, there were no signs of her identity about her body. Whoever had killed her made sure to remove any forms of ID. Why would someone want her dead? And what possible link did she have to the first victim?

He ducked beneath the cordon tape and followed the curve of the bridge as it curled around on itself and then straightened to cross the road. Metal bars ran the length on both sides.

He came to a halt in the same place both the victim and her killer would have been before she'd died. A cold wind rippled through his hair and whipped his tie out from his shirt. He tucked it between two of the buttons and did up his jacket. His eyes watered at the chill, and if he stayed up here long enough, he'd end up with an earache.

The bridge railings came up to the middle of his chest. They'd been built high enough to prevent anyone accidentally falling.

He wanted to place his gloved hands on the metal, to see how difficult it would be to pull himself up, but he didn't want to destroy any evidence. SOCO had already dusted the railings, but there might be prints they hadn't yet lifted.

What he could tell was that it wouldn't be easy to get someone over the top. It wasn't as though they could just be pushed. They'd have needed to pick up the victim and throw them over, which would have taken some strength.

Just like with the first victim, who must have been carried or at least helped some distance across the fields, from the road, to reach the train track, it pointed towards their perpetrator being a man—a physically strong one at that. In Ryan's mind, the killer was younger, most likely below fifty or even forty, probably tall and well built, and in good shape.

What reason did the killer have for choosing these two particular victims? They were both white and of a similar age, but so far that was all they had. He found it hard to believe it had been done at random, but it was a possibility. They might have just been in the wrong place at the wrong time.

The act of cutting out a tongue and sewing lips together felt personal to him, though. It was deliberate, a way of sending a message. Perhaps the message was to someone not even connected to the victims?

The frustration of not yet knowing the answer gnawed at him. These were the kinds of questions that would keep him awake at night. It was his job to find out the answers, and he wouldn't rest until he did.

Chapter Fourteen

Ryan was going to need to bring more detectives in.

Now, they not only had investigations ongoing into the first murder, but they also had to follow up on a second. It didn't help that one of his constables had no experience and so didn't bring a whole lot to the team. DC Grewal was doing his best, and Ryan appreciated that, but he needed someone who didn't need their hand held.

Back in the office, he went to his DCI to request the extra support.

DCI Hirst agreed. "I'll see what I can do."

"Thank you. We still don't know exactly where the first victim was taken from, or even how, or where the killer takes them to mutilate their mouths like that. Currently, we have more questions than answers."

"Do you have an ID on the second victim?"

"Not yet, but I suspect someone is going to miss her soon, especially when the news breaks about a woman of her age being killed. There was no way we could keep the press away from such a big scene, though. Of course, they won't know the details. The good news is that we've at least got a witness report that claims to have seen the killer. I'm hoping we'll have some dashcam footage soon, too, that will have caught him. Even if we can get a vague description, it'll be something."

"Keep me updated, and I'll let you know if we can pull in some more resources from other teams."

"Thanks, boss," he said and left the room.

He brought his team up to speed on the most recent developments.

"Thank you for all your hard work on this, folks," he told them. "I know you've already got your hands full, and now I'm asking you to do even more. Right now, it would seem that we're dealing with the same perpetrator responsible for killing Gary Carter."

"You don't think it might be a copycat?" Shonda asked from her desk.

"I think it's unlikely. We haven't released the details of the first case to the public yet, but considering how many people were on that train, it's possible someone saw the victim's face and leaked it." He tapped his finger to his lips, thinking out loud. "Both scenes also had multiple witnesses. Does the killer crave an audience?"

Linda called over, "Will the pathologist be able to tell if it was the same person who sewed up their lips?"

Ryan nodded. "I believe so, yes, and hopefully forensics will be able to match the thread, too." He carried on. "We still haven't found Carter's car, so I need someone to focus on that. Let's get some drones up around the area between where he went missing and the train tracks where he died. Finding the vehicle might unlock some vital clues."

"I can take that, boss," Dev volunteered.

Ryan nodded his thanks to his constable.

"Right now, we have the driver confirming that two people were standing on top of the bridge right before the victim fell.

With any luck, someone will have caught the killer's face on camera."

Linda Quinn half lifted a hand to ask a question. "If the victim was just standing up there, was she also drugged? I mean, we know Gary Carter had enough drugs in his system to fell a horse, but if she was standing, does that mean she wasn't drugged?"

"That's a good point," Ryan said. "The right dose of Rohypnol could make it so the victim was still able to walk but would be compliant, unlike the victim on the train track. It's not an easy thing to get right, however. They must have known what they were doing."

"Are we looking for someone with a medical background, perhaps," Linda suggested. "They cut out the victim's tongue, cauterised the wound, and sewed their mouths shut. Could they have medical training?"

Ryan grimaced. "Possibly, though the pathologist didn't think the cuts or stitches were professional enough to be a surgeon."

"Okay, not a surgeon then. But if they have experience with Rohypnol..."

She left the question hanging in the air, but he shook his head.

"I hate to say it, but anyone could have experience with Rohypnol these days. If someone wanted to experiment with doses, they could easily do that by going into pubs and clubs and picking on some unsuspecting victim. They could watch the victim's reactions, without actually doing anything to them, and decide if they need more or less to meet their needs."

"Wouldn't the person report it?" Linda said.

"Maybe, but often people just think they drank way too much or make up other excuses to themselves. It only stays in the system for twenty-four hours, so by the time they've come to the conclusion they were drugged, it's often too late to prove it." Linda had a point, though, and he considered this for a moment. "Okay, can you go back over any recent cases of people reporting spiking—men and women, because we know our killer has targeted both, and I imagine they'd want to know how it affected both sexes. See if there's any pattern that crops up. If they were in certain pubs or clubs, we might even be able to catch them on CCTV."

He knew it was a long shot, but sometimes these things came up with the goods.

"I'll check into it," she said.

Ryan worked through the rest of his team, ensuring he had someone covering each aspect of the investigation. Though he always wanted to be as involved as possible in a case, it was his job to oversee his team and make sure things were getting done. Just like with the first murder, they needed to find out the identity of the victim as a priority.

Mallory called over to him from her desk. "Boss, I've got dashcam footage from one of the vehicles."

"Excellent. Have you watched it yet?"

"No, it literally just arrived in my inbox."

He hoped this would be the breakthrough they needed.

"Let's take a look then."

He joined her at her desk as she downloaded the video footage and then brought it up on screen to watch. They knew what time the incident had happened so were able to fast forward to where they needed to be, moments before the crash.

The car with the dashcam moved through traffic, switching lanes, so they had the view of the vehicles ahead and their licence plates.

"Make a note of those and run them," Ryan said. "If they were ahead of the lorry when the crash happened, they could be witnesses we haven't managed to track down yet."

"Good thinking."

"It might be worth doing a media appeal as well," he said, mainly thinking out loud. "Finding out who was near the area at the time of the incident, and if they saw anything. In particular, it would be helpful to find anyone else who might have used the bridge when the killer and the victim were already up there, or perhaps on their way up. Someone could have walked right by them and not even realised who they were."

"Agreed."

Ryan turned his attention back to the screen. The vehicle was almost at the location of the accident now. He watched, waiting for the bridge to come into view.

He pointed at the screen. "There, stop."

She clicked on the mouse to pause the footage.

The shot was from a distance. The position of the camera on the dashboard meant that the closer the car got to the bridge, the less of it they were able to view. The lorry was still several cars ahead, but it was on the inside lane so wasn't blocking the view.

They'd paused on a section where they were able to see both people standing on the bridge.

Ryan studied the image. "We need to zoom in on them and then get it cleaned up. We can't see much from that."

Mallory leaned in closer. "We can get confirmation of the killer's height, though, and body shape. They've got a hood up to hide their face, but from what I can tell, he's Caucasian."

Ryan agreed. "If digital forensics are able to make the picture any clearer, we might be able to get a few more details."

"Anything will help at this point."

Mallory exhaled a breath and sat back. "The poor woman. I can't imagine what must have been going through her mind. Did she have any idea what was happening to her, or was she completely out of it?"

"Let's hope it's the latter."

What must it be like to have your tongue cut out and your lips sewn together? She couldn't scream or call for help. The killer literally took her voice from her. Maybe that's why he did it? Ryan had been focused on the likelihood that it had been sending a message, but perhaps it was a more practical act, a way of stopping their victims from calling for help?

He told Mallory his thoughts.

She considered this. "It still seems like an extreme way of achieving such a thing. What's wrong with a piece of duct tape?"

Ryan couldn't help grinning. "Everyone's doing duct tape these days. Maybe he wants to stand out from the crowd."

"A trend-setter."

"Let's hope not."

They both chuckled.

"Do you think there might be a third victim?" Mallory asked.

"Not if we can stop him first. We need to find out the connection between these two victims, if there is one."

"We don't even know this victim's name yet, never mind if there's a connection."

"No, but we will. Someone is going to miss her. I'm sure of it."

They went back to the video footage, watching it right to the point of the crash. The moment the victim was thrown from the bridge wasn't visible on the dashcam, but the carnage that followed when she hit the lorry was. It all happened so fast. One moment, the car was driving along, the next it was spinning, with flashes of other vehicles in front of it, and then the screen went blank.

"The killer must have run the second he threw her," Ryan said. "He was relying on the chaos he'd just caused to ensure no one stopped or noticed him."

"He could only have gone one of two ways, though. I find it hard to believe no one saw him."

Ryan gritted his teeth. "So far, no one saw him take her up there either. How was that even possible when she had her mouth sewn up like that? He must have been pretty confident he wasn't going to meet someone walking in the opposite direction. It would have been noticed."

"Or he had her face covered," Mallory suggested. "The wind was cold today. Could he have wrapped a scarf or something around the lower part of her face to keep it hidden? If he walked with his arm around her, they might have appeared more natural."

"Possibly. Or the killer is just a cocky son of a bitch who believes they won't be caught."

She angled her head. "Or that."

"Was a scarf or anything found at the scene?"

Mallory nodded. "Yes, the victim was wearing one. Not one of the thick woollen ones, but the thinner chiffon material."

"You're right. I remember." He exhaled air through his nose. "It's a possibility he did use that to cover her face then."

"We might be able to tell more from the footage."

"Get it over to digital forensics, see if they can clean it up for us. A description of a woman with a scarf covering her face might be remembered by someone."

Chapter Fifteen

Olwen couldn't concentrate. A storm raged in her head, and she couldn't quieten it.

At work, she wrote numbers in the wrong columns and sent an email to one client that was meant for someone else. She had to apologise profusely, realising she'd sent confidential information to someone who wasn't the client. If she wasn't careful, those kinds of mistakes could cost her her job.

She couldn't shake what Andy and the others had implied.

Had there really been abuse happening at the foster home? Who had been responsible? Was that the reason the place had been shut down and they'd moved?

She took a few minutes out of her lunch break to do a Google search, putting in everything she could think of to pull up the address of the old foster home. But it had been the nineties, and it wasn't like now, where every little detail of everything was put online. Wouldn't the local newspapers have reported on it, though?

The part that disturbed her the most was that it had been happening right under her nose and she'd been completely clueless. Why had no one ever said anything to her? They'd clearly spoken to each other about it. She assumed it was because she was the daughter of the people running the place. Somehow, she'd managed to convince herself that she was one of them—just one of the foster kids—but of course she hadn't been. She'd believed they'd been her friends, but had they always looked at her differently? The rich little girl living next door trying to be one of them?

It had been thirty years, but she still found herself cringing inside. Had they laughed about her, talked about her behind her back? The idea that they'd all just been humouring her was absolutely mortifying.

Whatever had been going on at the foster home, it had been well covered up. There was nothing online about it, not even reported rumours or suspicions. Was it possible that Andy was wrong? Maybe they were just spiteful rumours to get the place shut down. But then she thought of Philip. How could they just be rumours if they'd driven a boy to kill himself?

The memory of that brown-eyed boy with the freckles flashed into her head. He'd been quiet, but funny, too, always the prankster. How could she not have known that something so terrible had been happening to him? But all those kids had suffered some kind of pain, hadn't they? After all, they were in a foster home for a reason. They all came from abusive backgrounds and broken homes. They were there because their families either couldn't or wouldn't take care of them.

She couldn't remember what kind of home Phillip had come from. Wasn't it possible that he'd been in an abusive home and the stories he'd told the others were actually things that had happened to him before he'd been placed there? One thing those kids needed more than anything was attention. Perhaps that's all Phillip had been trying to get. The attention of the others. Making up stories of abuse was certainly one way of getting it.

But then why go on and kill himself?

The damage that had been done to him before arriving at the foster home might have been too great. Maybe he'd never got over it.

As much as Olwen wanted to believe what she was telling herself, she still needed desperately to speak to the people who'd been involved in her childhood. She wanted to see her father. It probably wouldn't do any good—he couldn't remember who she was half the time, never mind what had happened thirty years ago. Maybe she just wanted to purge herself of these thoughts.

She was due a visit to see him anyway. Perhaps she'd ask him, just to find out if he remembered.

On her desk, Olwen's phone buzzed with a message. She picked it up and checked the screen. It was from Andy.

I'm sorry if we upset you last night.

Her heart immediately beat harder, as though it was trying to hammer its way out of her ribcage. Her hands trembled, and she couldn't catch her breath. She shouldn't reply. What good would come of it?

She guessed that time living next to the foster home had been her 'coming of age' period, where she'd gone from being a young girl to having her eyes opened up to the world as a young woman. She'd be the first to admit that she had enjoyed being 'led astray' as people said. When cans of cider were offered to her, quickly followed up by cigarettes, and then spliffs of marijuana, she'd found the whole thing dangerous and exciting.

Olwen thought of Helen, who'd been her best friend at school. Helen would be able to give Olwen her honest opinion about the place, wouldn't she? She'd spent time at the foster home as well.

She hadn't been in touch with her friend for several years. Could she just phone her out of the blue? She wasn't even completely sure that she had the right number for her anymore. They'd grown apart since those later years in secondary school, though Olwen had never really understood the reason. She guessed it was just one of those natural things. They'd reconnected on social media and had seen each other a handful of times, but it was hard staying in touch with people when you were in your forties. Everyone seemed to have such busy lives.

Olwen scrolled through her phone until she got to Helen's name. Her stomach churned with nerves at the idea of hitting the 'call' button. Why was she nervous? Was it because she was worried Helen wouldn't want to hear from her? Or was it because she was worried about what her old friend might say?

She decided to just do it. If she didn't, it would only be playing on her mind.

She hit 'call' and put the phone to her ear.

Helen answered, sounding delighted at hearing from her.

"Oh my God, Olwen. How long has it been? I've been meaning to phone you. I'm so sorry I'm such a rubbish friend."

Olwen gave a small laugh. "Don't be silly. I haven't phoned you either. I know how it is. Time just gets away, doesn't it?" She felt a little guilty that she was phoning for a reason and not just because she wanted to chat.

"No, listen, the reason I'd been planning to call you is that I'm in Bristol. I'm here on a course. Are you free? I can meet for coffee, if you fancy it? Or maybe wine?"

Olwen hadn't been expecting that. Helen had moved to Surrey several years earlier, which had been part of the reason they'd fallen out of touch. She'd been preparing herself for a phone conversation but nothing more.

"I'd love that. When are you free?"

"How about after work?" Helen suggested.

Olwen's stomach flipped with fresh nerves. "After work sounds great."

Chapter Sixteen

"Boss, we've got an ID on our female victim," Dev Patel said as he approached Ryan's desk. "She's sixty-four-year-old Jillian Griffiths. She works as a customer service manager for an insurance company."

"Good work. Is she married?" he asked. "Any children?"

"Widowed, and two children who are grown—Caroline Feeny and Lee Griffiths. They're the ones who reported her missing."

"Any priors?"

He sucked air in over his teeth and shook his head. "Nope. Clean as a whistle. Her daughter, Caroline, reported her missing after she didn't show up for coffee like she was supposed to. She rang her phone, but obviously got no answer, and then went around to her house and she wasn't there. She checked with all the friends and neighbours, but no one had seen her. The daughter gave it a few hours, and when her mother still hadn't shown up, she called us, and we were able to match the description."

"Have we had a definite ID yet?"

"We haven't run a DNA match yet, but from the photograph the daughter was able to show us, it's clearly the same woman."

"Have the family been informed about the nature of her death?" Ryan asked.

"Uniform have told them that she died after falling from a bridge and being hit by a lorry, but not any of the details, such as that we suspect this is murder or about the sewn mouth."

Ryan got to his feet and called across the office to get the attention of his team.

"Everyone, we've got the ID of the second victim, a Mrs Jillian Griffiths." He filled them in with her date of birth and current address. "We need to focus our attention on two things. Firstly, I want to know Jillian Griffith's final movements. We know she was abducted long enough for someone to mutilate her, so where did the killer take her from and when? The more we can narrow that down, the more likely it is that we're going to be able to find out who did it. We're going to need bank and phone records, and talk to anyone she may have had contact with between her last time being in contact with her daughter and her being thrown from that bridge." He paused for breath.

"So, was she taken from her home?" Mallory asked.

"That's what we need to find out. Let's get permission from the family to search the place. Secondly, we need to find out if there's a connection between the two victims. Did they know each other? Compare their phone records and bank statements. Were they ever in the same location at the same time? Did they shop at the same places? Eat in the same restaurants? Do they have any memberships to anywhere that are the same? There has to be something."

He could feel himself becoming more impassioned about the case with every word. This was a puzzle he was determined to solve.

"I want everything from both crime scenes evaluated. Let's compare all the car licence plates we have from both scenes. I know there's not many from the first one, but that should only make it easier to find a link. Whoever brought the victim to the bridge must have had a mode of transport. If they'd been on foot for too long, someone would have spotted them."

A murmur of agreement rose from his team.

"Then there is the sewing up of the lips," Ryan continued. "It has to mean something. Whoever is doing this is trying to get a message out, but what?"

One of his constables, Shonda, spoke up. "Could they have been having an affair and the sewn mouths are some kind of punishment? Like for keeping secrets or something."

He considered her suggestion. "That's a pretty drastic way of punishing someone for an affair, plus Jillian Griffiths was a widow, and Gary Carter was separated, and had been for six months, so technically, they wouldn't have been wronging anyone if they were involved with each other." He turned to his sergeant. "Mallory, since you interviewed the family of the first victim, it would be a good idea if you speak to the second victim's as well. Something might resonate with you and help us figure out what's connecting the two victims."

"Isn't it possible that there is no link?" she asked.

Ryan shook his head. "Even when killers believe they're choosing a victim at random, something is pushing them to pick one person over another. Find out if Jillian was involved with anyone, and if they know the name Gary Carter. There's a link, we just have to find it."

Chapter Seventeen

An hour later, Mallory found herself sitting in the victim's living room. She'd donned protective boots and gloves, and SOCO would be arriving shortly, as this was now a potential crime scene.

The daughter, Caroline Feeny, was there with her brother, Lee. Caroline had a key to the victim's home and had gone there to check on her mother. She'd wanted to wait there for her mother to come home, except she hadn't, and then Caroline hadn't been able to bring herself to leave. Uniformed officers had already informed them of their mother's death.

The news had clearly come as a shock.

The room was tidy and tastefully decorated in greys and creams, with the occasional pop of colour. Mallory was sure she recognised the set of gold-wire shelves attached to the wall as being from B&M.

"I'm so sorry for your loss," Mallory told them both.

The young woman wept openly. Her brother sat with his arm around her shoulders, his face pale, his lips pinched.

"I believe my colleagues informed you about your mother's death this morning?"

"They told us she fell from a bridge and was hit by a lorry," Lee said. "How is that even possible? Do they think that she jumped?"

Caroline sniffed. "She wasn't suicidal. No way. She was happy, and she'd never have done something like that to us. She loved us too much."

"We don't believe she committed suicide," Mallory said. "We don't think it was an accident either. I'm afraid to tell you that your mother's death is now officially a murder investigation."

The son straightened, his attention caught. "You're saying someone pushed her?"

Mallory nodded. "Yes. I'm terribly sorry, but we believe that's what happened."

The victim's daughter covered her face with her hands. "Oh God. Someone killed Mum?"

Lee held Mallory's gaze. "Why would someone do that to her? She never hurt anyone in her life."

"That's what we're working to find out. When was the last time you saw your mother?"

"On Sunday. We still come around for a roast dinner." Fresh tears sprang in her eyes. "That's never going to happen again. I can't believe it."

"How did she seem then?"

Caroline wiped tears from her cheeks. "She was fine. Completely normal."

"Nothing bothering her? She didn't mention anything different?"

"No, nothing like that. We just had a normal Sunday lunch and left here about five, with promises to meet for coffee during the week."

"She wasn't in any trouble that you know of?" Mallory asked. "No drinking or gambling or debts...anything like that?"

Lee blinked at her. "What? Our mother? No, not at all. She was a normal woman in her sixties. She didn't get involved with anything like that."

"What about her work? Was she happy there? Any problems?"

He stared at her like she was crazy. "She worked part-time in insurance. In an office."

"Do you have the number of her manager at all? Just so we can get in touch?"

"I'm sure I can find it."

Caroline took her brother's hand. "Someone's targeted her? That's what you're saying. Whoever did this chose her on purpose?"

"Again, we don't know that for sure yet. It might have been a case of her being in the wrong place at the wrong time."

Lee shook his head. "This is crazy. I can't believe this is happening. It's a fucking nightmare I need someone to wake me up from."

"Do you know if your mother was seeing anyone else at all? Did she have a man in her life?"

"I don't think there's been anyone serious," Caroline said. "Our dad died three years ago, which isn't that long really. She loved our father. They'd been together for almost forty years when he died. She's never been interested in anyone else, has she, Lee?"

Her brother responded. "No. What did she need a man around for? She had us."

Mallory got the impression the two of them had slightly blinkered ideas about the reason their mother might have wanted to meet someone else, but then perhaps they were right, and Jillian hadn't been interested. She was only in her sixties, though. Surely it would have been natural for her to want someone else in her life.

"Anyway," Lee continued, clearly irritated. "Why are you asking about her bloody love life? Shouldn't you be trying to find out who did this?"

Mallory remained calm. "Motive is an important aspect in solving a crime, Mr Griffiths, and unfortunately, many women are murdered by the men in their lives. It's a line of questioning I have to ask."

The son gave a strange kind of laugh. "So what? You think she met a man, and he killed her?"

It made Mallory think of Daniel. Why did men who'd never experienced violence not believe women or think they were overexaggerating? Did they even think women deserved it? That they were 'asking for it' or needed to be 'put in their place'?

A familiar anger rose inside her, and she quashed it down. She was letting her personal experiences and feelings cloud her judgement. There was no reason for this man to think that way. He'd just lost his mother. She was sure he was more than aware of the violence of men against women.

"It's possible, yes. We really do need to look at all possibilities right now."

Lee's lips thinned. "You should be focusing more on what happened on that bridge. People must have seen whoever pushed her. If they were standing above a fucking road with four lanes, there must have been loads of cars that passed beneath them. The drivers must have seen something!"

"We have officers interviewing all possible witnesses."

He threw up his hands, growing more agitated by the second. "And how did the driver of that lorry not stop? He must have seen her there."

"It really was impossible. There was nowhere near enough time. He tried, and it caused a multiple car pileup behind him. A number of people were taken to hospital."

He pressed the balls of his hands into his eye sockets. "Jesus Christ."

"The driver of the lorry is devastated about what happened."

It wasn't fair of them to blame the driver, but she understood that need to lash out at someone. To have someone to blame. Right now, they didn't have the killer to aim their grief at, so the driver would have to do.

Mallory linked her fingers between her knees and took a breath. The son and daughter didn't even know the full extent of what their mother had gone through yet, but it was important she be open with them.

"There's something else I need to tell you, and I'm afraid this may be distressing to hear."

The brother and sister glanced at each other and took each other's hands again, squeezing tight.

"What is it?" he asked. "Please, just tell us."

"The main reason we're treating this as a murder case is because your mother's lips had been sewn together, and we have reason to believe her tongue may have been cut out before she was killed."

What little colour remained in the daughter's face quickly drained. "Oh no. Please, no. I think I'm going to pass out."

Sure enough, her eyes flickered, the irises disappearing, replaced by bloodshot whites. Her brother moved behind her, supporting her back, and laying her down on the sofa.

"Do we need to call a paramedic?" Mallory asked.

"No, it's okay. She has a habit of fainting. She'll come round in a minute."

"I'll get her some water."

Mallory got to her feet and went into the kitchen. It took her a couple of doors before she found the cabinet with the glassware. She selected a sturdy tumbler and carried it over to the sink and ran the tap until the water was cold.

She took a minute to herself before filling it. Delivering that kind of news was always distressing. She hung her head and blew out a breath and then focused on filling the glass.

As she turned, her gaze caught on a paper calendar hanging on the wall. Every other square box had something scribbled in it with pen. It was difficult to read what was written, but it might help them narrow down the victim's movements on the days preceding her death. The killer might have seen her at one of the appointments and decided she'd be his next victim.

Using her phone, Mallory took a photograph of the calendar.

She returned to the living room. As Lee had predicted, Caroline had already come around and was sitting up on the sofa, her face in her hands. Mallory handed her the tumbler of water. Caroline took a sip, her hands shaking.

Mallory felt bad that she was having to drag them through this, instead of leaving them alone with their grief, but it was her job. Besides, assuming they caught the person who'd done this, the family would hear all the gory details in court.

"I'm sorry to keep pressing you for information," she said, "but the hours and days after a murder can be some of the most important in finding who did this."

Lee nodded. "It's okay. We understand."

"I just noticed your mother had the initials R.G. written on her calendar on the day before she died. Do you have any idea what they stand for?"

The siblings exchanged a glance to see if the other one knew, but they both shook their heads.

Lee pursed his lips. "No, sorry. Doesn't mean anything."

"She didn't mention having plans that day to either of you?"

Again, she was only rewarded with the shaking of heads.

Mallory craned her head to see out of the living room window to where a small red Ford Fiesta sat on the driveway. "Is that your mother's car?"

Lee followed her line of sight and nodded. "Yes, it is."

"I'd like to get forensics on it, dust it for prints. There might be a chance her killer was in her car at some point. We'll be doing the same with the house, if that's okay? Do you have somewhere else you can go while it's being done?"

"Of course. Do whatever you need."

Mallory turned her attention back to Caroline. "You said in your missing person's report that you'd tried to call her mobile. Do you have any idea what happened to her phone? Did she tend to carry a handbag as well?"

"Yes, she did. She always had both her phone and her handbag with her."

They hadn't yet recovered those items. Mallory wondered if the killer had taken them.

"Did she have any other devices? A computer or laptop?"

"She has an iPad. She's always on that thing." Caroline's face fell. "Was, I mean. She was always on it."

"Is there any chance you know her PIN or password for it?"

"I can take a good guess as to what it might be. Do you think there might be something on it that'll point to whoever killed her?"

Mallory offered her a sympathetic smile. "I'm unsure yet, but it'll definitely be worth checking. We'll also request her phone and bank details, see if we can retrace her footsteps before she died." She moved on to a slightly different line of questioning. "When you arrived at her house, you let yourself in with a key, is that correct?"

"Yes, that's right. It was about midday."

"The door was locked then?" Mallory checked.

Fresh worry tightened Caroline's features. "Yes, it was."

"Did you notice any signs of disturbances? Did your mother have anything like a Ring doorbell or any other CCTV?"

"No. Sorry."

"That's okay," Mallory said. "We'll speak with the neighbours. Hopefully, someone will have one and we'll be able to catch when your mother left her house for the final time."

More and more people were getting their own security these days. Mostly, it was to spy on delivery drivers to make sure they got their packages than for any kind of serious crime, but it all came in handy.

Mallory linked her fingers together, her elbows on her knees. "I have one last question, at least for the moment. Do you know the name Gary Carter at all?"

Lee's forehead furrowed, and he turned to his sister. "It doesn't mean anything to me. What about you, Caroline?"

"No, I don't recognise it. Why? Do you think he might be the person responsible for killing our mother?"

Mallory shook her head. They were going to find out soon enough. "We're currently investigating the possibility that there was a previous victim."

Lee's jaw dropped. "You mean someone has done this before?"

"Gary Carter was hit by a train a few days ago. Like with your mother, his lips had been sewn together."

"What does that mean?" Caroline asked.

"We're not sure yet. It's still early days in the investigation."

The siblings appeared understandably horrified. It was hard enough to lose a parent, but doing so under such violent circumstances made everything worse. Mallory's heart went out to them. She was lucky in that both her parents were still alive, and she dreaded the thought of anything happening to either of them. She couldn't imagine how Ollie would cope either. He'd never lost someone he loved.

Chapter Eighteen

On the incident board, photographs of the two victims, and the details of the crime scenes, had been placed side by side.

Ryan turned to his sergeant, who was half sitting, half leaning on a desk on the other side of the room. She'd just got back from speaking to the second victim's family and fed back everything she'd learned. One ankle was hooked over the other, and she used her hands to prop herself up.

"What is it that's connecting these two people," Ryan said, "because there has to be something. I'm sure the sewn lips are sending a message, and I highly doubt that whoever has chosen the victims has done so at random."

Mallory chewed at her lower lip as she thought. "They were of a similar sort of age. They're both from Bristol." She let out a breath. "Other than that, we've got nothing."

"We need to dig deeper. There has to be something."

"They weren't even in a similar area when they went missing," Mallory said. "One was south of the city, the other in the north. They are both Bristol born and bred, though."

Ryan considered this for a moment. "Let's go back farther. Where did they go to school? Where have they worked in the past? Who are their families? There must be some kind of connection."

He pressed his knuckles to his lips. It was incredibly frustrating that he couldn't figure out what tied the victims together. Right now, they just looked like two random people from different parts of the city, but he knew that couldn't be the case. Even murders that appeared to be random, normally weren't, and the MO of the lips being sewn was too specific for this to be a case of being in the wrong place at the wrong time. There had to be a link.

Mallory took her phone from her pocket. "I did see something on the calendar in Jillian's kitchen. I snapped a photograph."

She straightened and brought the phone over to him. "It's hard to know what it means." Mallory spread two fingers on the screen to make the image bigger. "It's just two initials: R.G."

"Did the family have any idea what the initials stood for?"

"Nope. I already asked them."

"If Jillian went out the evening before she died, that could easily have been when she was abducted."

"We've taken Jillian's iPad and handed it over to digital forensics," Mallory said. "With any luck, they'll find something on it that will give us a better idea about what R.G. might stand for."

"Good. What about her bank records? Any sign of her cards being used?"

"No. The last time she used her card was to pay for parking near where she works. According to her colleagues, she left at five-thirty, and she was acting normally."

"And her phone data? Where was the last ping from?"

"Near her home on the evening before she died. We know she was driving when she left work, because she paid for parking, and her car is on the driveway at home, so we know she made it back to her house. There are no signs of anyone breaking in. The daughter had to use her key to gain entry, so the place was all locked up."

Ryan was putting together the victim's final movements in his mind. "So somewhere between her leaving work at five-thirty the previous day, and being killed shortly after eight the following morning, she was abducted. Have we spoken to the neighbours? Did any of them see her coming or going that day? Any luck with them having security cameras?"

Mallory grimaced. "I'm afraid they must be the least observant street ever because no one saw anything, and we can't find anyone with a Ring doorbell or anything similar."

"Damn." He tapped his fingers against the side of his thigh. "She most likely left her house voluntarily that evening and didn't take her car. Did someone pick her up? Did she walk to meet whoever R.G. is?"

"Could R.G. even be the killer?"

He exhaled and rubbed his hand across his mouth. "If so, it means her killer was known to her. Could that be the same with Gary Carter as well? Did he know whoever put him on that train track?"

"It's a possibility."

"We know that Gary Carter was last seen at a small convenience store on the outskirts of the city, but we have footage of him getting back into his car and driving off. The vehicle is still missing. Does the killer have it? It hasn't been picked up on any ANPR cameras, so I don't think anyone is driving it around."

"We could really do with finding that vehicle," Mallory said.

Ryan nodded slowly and bit at his lower lip. "There's one thing that's really bothering me. Where is the killer taking his victims to mutilate them? How are they not being seen or heard?"

The ringing of his phone drew his attention, and he took it from his pocket.

Nikki's name appeared onscreen.

"It's Nikki," he said to his sergeant. "I'll need to take this."

Mallory nodded to show she'd understood and went back to her desk.

Nikki had been working on Jillian Griffiths. He hoped she had some information for him.

He swiped to answer. "Hi, Nikki. How's it going?"

"Good. I've been working on your second victim."

"I'm sorry, I don't have time to come down to the mortuary right now," he said. "I've got my hands full."

"It's not a problem. Everything is in my report, though I knew you'd want to hear it from me directly as well."

"I appreciate that. What are your thoughts?"

"It's the same killer," she said.

"You're sure?"

"Yes. The stitching of the mouth is identical, and though I've sent the thread off to the lab for confirmation, I believe it's the same kind of thread used, too. Like with the first victim, the tongue is missing. From the length and depth of the incisions, I believe the same blade was used in both cases. The tongue had also been cauterised."

"The chances of it being a copycat killer are slim to none," he said.

"Exactly. You're looking for the same person."

"Anything else that might help?"

"There was, actually. I found fibres in the victim's hair."

Ryan frowned and pressed the phone closer to his ear. "What kind of fibres?"

"Woodwool. I found three separate strands."

"The same fibres were found at the scene of the first victim. I'm not sure how useful it is knowing the victims and the killer have come into contact with them though. From the research I did on the fibres, they're widely used."

"They are," she said, "but there are different grades which are used for different things. Again, I've sent them off to the lab, but I'd suggest you get them to look into the fibres a little more deeply, see if you can narrow it down."

"I will, thanks. We didn't know the fibres from the first scene even had anything to do with the killer, so we didn't look into it that hard. I'll make sure that changes." Ryan moved on. "What about drugs? Was there Rohypnol in the victim's system?"

"Yes, though not in as high levels as with the first victim. It was used to sedate her, however. It's definitely the same MO."

"Thanks, Nikki."

Ryan ended the call and went out to address the rest of his team. "I know it's getting late, everyone, but we've had confirmation from the pathologist that we're dealing with the same killer for both victims." He hadn't really been expecting anything different. "We need to find someone who is an expert in woodwool. Fibres have been found at both scenes now. It's got a wide usage, but it also comes in various grades, depending on the use. Can we find someone who knows their stuff? If the fibres are being picked up from the location where he's taking the victims to mutilate them, it might narrow our search down."

"I'll get on the phone," said the new recruit, DC Grewal. "See who I can find."

"Thanks. It might be that they don't mean anything, but at this point we need to follow up on all the leads we have."

Chapter Nineteen

Olwen had arranged to meet Helen at one of the popular wine bars in the centre of the city. It made sense for them to go somewhere close by the hotel where Helen was staying.

Her friend hadn't arrived yet, so Olwen ordered a bottle of Sauvignon Blanc and asked for a couple of glasses. Helen had never been one to turn down a glass of wine.

Olwen grabbed a table and poured her own drink, sipping at it nervously while keeping an eye on the door. Her heart lurched each time someone entered but then sank again when it wasn't her.

She checked her phone in case Helen had messaged her to say she'd been caught up in something and was running late, or that she needed to cancel, but there was nothing.

The alcohol heated her cheeks, and she realised she'd almost finished the glass already.

Movement came at the entrance, and she glanced back over to see Helen appear. She paused for a moment, peering around, and then caught sight of Olwen. A wide smile spread across Helen's face, and she hurried over.

Olwen got to her feet, grinning back. She gave a squeal of delight and hugged her old friend.

"You always look exactly the same," Helen said, holding her at an arm's length so she could see her better.

Self-conscious, Olwen smoothed down her hair. "God, no I don't. I'm getting old. I'm practically grey now, or at least I would be beneath the hair dye. You look great, though."

"Thanks. I finally lost the baby weight. Only took me twelve years."

They both laughed.

"Sit down," Olwen said. "I bought a bottle. I hope that's all right."

"Absolutely. I'll get the next one."

Olwen thought she might be on her backside by the second bottle. She set about pouring Helen a glass and then topping up her own.

They made small talk for a while, catching up on each other's lives. Olwen experienced a twinge of guilt that she'd lured Helen here on false pretences. While Helen thought they were just here as old friends, Olwen had a motive.

She allowed what she hoped was a reasonable amount of time to pass before she waited for a pause in the conversation where she could jump in with her reason for being there.

"Do you remember the house my parents ran? The one next door to mine."

Instantly, Helen's expression changed, morphing into a mask. "Why are you asking about that?"

"I bumped into one of the boys—well, he's a man now—who used to live there. He said something strange about something that happened..."

"Why would I know anything about that?"

"I don't know." She thought about it for a moment. "I guess because you came over a few times as well when it first opened, and then all of a sudden, I didn't see you as much.

You stopped coming round, and it felt like we were distant at school. It literally only just occurred to me that it might have been because of that place."

Helen didn't meet her eye, swirling her finger in the condensation on the outside of her glass. "I guess it was. After it opened, you were there all the time, and I just didn't want to be, so I stayed away."

"I wasn't there all the time."

"Yes, you were. It was like you moved in, too. You were always in one of their rooms."

Olwen pressed her lips into a thin line and shook her head. "No, my parents would never have allowed it."

Helen scoffed. "I don't think your parents were paying much attention. That's why they had people working there—so they didn't have to get involved."

It had been a different time back then. In the nineties, parents didn't keep track of their kids the way they did now. There were no mobile phones, so kids said they were going out and they'd be back at a certain time, and that was it. Parents had no idea where they were during those times. She didn't think it was just her parents at fault.

"So, is that why we stopped hanging out?" Olwen asked. "Because I was always at the foster home?"

"Pretty much, yeah."

The realisation felt like a rock being dropped into the pit of her belly. "Shit, Helen. I'm sorry. I was a really shit friend, wasn't I? I'm surprised you're even still talking to me."

Helen shrugged. "You were going through your own stuff. I was okay. We both made our choices."

Olwen allowed this to sink in.

"It's strange, you know," Olwen said eventually. "It's like I can only remember chunks of things from back then."

Helen gave a small laugh. "That's hardly surprising. It was thirty years ago. I can't say that I remember everything about my teenage years either."

"I just—" She wasn't sure how to phrase it.

"You just what?" Helen's expression crumpled. "You don't think something horrible happened to you back then, do you? Something to do with the foster house? Some of those kids were bad news, you know. It was part of the reason I stayed away."

Olwen found herself getting defensive. "They weren't bad news. And nothing happened to me. I was fine."

Helen's forehead creased. "Then what's this all about? Why are you even thinking about the foster home all these years later?"

Olwen told her about going for a drink with Andy and the others and what they'd said about Philip.

"That's terrible," Helen said. "I think I remember Philip. How awful."

Olwen agreed. "That's why I keep going over things in my mind, trying to figure out if I missed something."

"Do you think one of the helpers your father employed might have been responsible?"

"Honestly, I don't know."

Helen seemed to think for a moment. "Why don't you just ask Andy?"

Olwen bit on her lower lip, gnawing at a piece of dried skin until she tasted blood.

"I'm not sure. Maybe because a stupid little part of me feels responsible. It was my father who was running the place, after all. He was the one hiring those people. You'd have thought he'd have done background checks on them or something."

"I'm sure he did. None of it was your fault."

It wasn't only that, though. Olwen was embarrassed admitting the truth of how she felt, and she ducked her head, focusing on her drink.

"They all stayed in touch," she said. "Well, maybe not all of them, but some of them. They stayed in touch with each other but not with me. It just feels like there was a reason behind that. And why didn't I make more effort to stay in touch with them? If we were all such good friends, why didn't I make more of a fuss at being taken away from them?"

Helen shrugged. "They were fickle kids. You just moved on. How many people are still in touch with everyone they knew as teenagers? I know I'm definitely not."

She had a point.

"Anyway," Helen continued, "you have to remember that you weren't one of them. No matter how much time you spent with them, you always had a home to go back to. It's like that song we used to listen to by Pulp, do you remember? 'Common People'? No matter how much she tried to live like the others, she always had her father's money to fall back on. That safety net was always there. I expect that's how the foster kids saw you. You always had a home."

"You're right."

Helen twisted her lips. "You could always ask your dad?"

"Yeah, I've considered that, but he's not well. Alzheimer's. He went downhill after we lost Mum."

"I'm so sorry." She reached out and squeezed Olwen's hand. "You should have told me sooner. I feel so bad that you've been dealing with it all on your own."

"I've been fine, but I don't think he'd remember much about the foster home. It was just a blink in his lifetime."

"You never know. Sometimes patients recall things from their past more than they do their present."

Olwen nodded. That was true.

"Don't you have an aunt as well?" Helen said. "You could try talking to her?"

For some reason, it had never even occurred to her to talk to Aunt Millicent. She remembered how angry her aunt had been about her parents opening the home. Milly had never agreed with it, though at the time Olwen had thought that was because her aunt was being protective of her. If that was the case, however, why had her aunt just cut off her ties with them? Was it possible that she'd actually known something else?

Olwen nodded. "Thanks, Helen. You're right. I'll get in touch with her. I'm so glad we got to do this. I'll change the subject now."

But no matter what she said, that knot of unease inside her still hadn't released. She was sure something had happened in that house, a reason why her parents had moved and the place had been shut down.

She just wished she could remember what.

Chapter Twenty

Mallory had to leave work shortly after six. She and Ollie had an appointment over at the residential house where Oliver's friend lived, where they had a room come up free. The woman who oversaw the property had phoned her earlier that day to arrange the visit.

Mallory had almost told her it wasn't a good time and that she needed to work late, but then it hit her that this was exactly the sort of situation Oliver had been complaining about. There would always be another case, and, as long as she worked this job, it would mean Ollie would always be left on his own. Mallory had ambitions, too. While she couldn't see herself getting married and having children anytime soon, she did want to progress in her career. She couldn't see any reason why she wouldn't be working as a detective inspector herself one day, but that meant yet more responsibility and less time for her brother.

Mallory drove home and picked up Ollie to take him to the residential home.

"You excited?" she asked.

Oliver clapped. "Yes, really excited. I think I'm going to love it, Mallory."

"I hope so."

The property was only a twenty-minute drive from their house, but it felt like so much longer.

"We can still see each other every day, can't we?" Oliver asked as she drove.

"Of course we can, though you may end up too busy with all your friends to want to see me every day."

He considered this for a moment. "Every other day then."

She tried not to feel hurt at his easy acceptance of her not being constantly in his life. Oliver didn't normally like change, but he seemed to be accepting this with ease. She told herself it was because he was maturing socially now. He was in his twenties; of course he didn't want to be hanging on to her coattails anymore. People with Down's syndrome could live perfectly independent lives. Some even formed relationships and went on to get married. She would love for Oliver to have a sweetheart one day—nothing would make her happier than seeing him living a fulfilling and loving life.

She remembered what Ryan had said about her not holding Oliver back. If that was really what she wanted, she needed to be encouraging him to take these steps.

Mallory pulled the car up outside the address and turned off the engine. She turned to her brother. "Ready?"

He beamed. "Yeah."

They got out and approached the big, three-storey Victorian.

"I can ring the bell, Mallory," Oliver said, bounding up the steps to the front door.

He did, and they waited until a woman in her forties opened it.

"Oliver!" she greeted. "It's so good to see you again. Come in, both of you."

The house had a warm feeling the moment they walked through the door. Everywhere was brightly coloured and cheerful; artwork, clearly done by the residents, had been framed and hung on the walls.

The woman turned to Mallory. "You must be the big sister I've heard so much about."

"Yes, I'm Mallory."

"I'm Susanne Haynes."

The two women shook hands.

"Well, it's lovely to meet you, Mallory. Whenever I've met with Ollie, all he does is talk about you non-stop."

"I'm sure that's not true."

"Well, you and his latest puzzle." She threw Oliver a wink, and they both laughed.

Mallory found herself smiling.

"Oliver tells me you're a detective," she said as she led them through the house. "That must be an exciting job."

"Nowhere near as exciting as the television shows would have you believe," she replied. "We spend far more time behind a desk and at a computer than we do in car chases and stakeouts."

"I bet. Well, let me show you the house. Let's start with the common room."

They entered a light, spacious room. A couple of the residents were already hanging out. One of them was Oliver's friend, and he jumped to his feet to race over to them.

"Ollie, you came!" A little more shyly, he added, "Hi, Mallory."

"Hi, Paul," she said. "Thanks for inviting us to see your home."

"That's okay. I hope you like it."

"We do so far." Mallory smiled at her brother. "Don't we, Oliver?"

"It's really nice," Ollie agreed.

Susanne continued with the guided tour, taking them into each of the rooms.

"The kitchen is laid out to enable the residents to make their own meals," she said. "It is supervised. Some of the residents need more help than others, so we keep an eye on them via camera." She pointed to the corners of the room where security cameras blinked. "There are security alarms on the gas in case anything is accidentally left on."

"We had a fire in the house not so long ago," Mallory told her. "Just a silly accident, but it shook Ollie up for a while."

"That's understandable. Someone is always around if Ollie feels he needs some extra help in the kitchen. How does that sound, Ollie?"

Oliver grinned his goofy smile. "Good."

"We try to have family meals at least a couple of times a week, too, where we all eat together, and we take it in turns to cook."

Deep down, Mallory knew this was for the best. All those times she thought of Oliver eating a sandwich at home on his own because she was having to work late wouldn't apply anymore. Ryan was right when he said it would give her some freedom, but to do what? She was frightened of being lonely and coming back to an empty house. Maybe she could think about renting a room out, but then she immediately dismissed the thought. If she couldn't even bring someone else in to replace Daniel for a few hours a week, how was she going to bring herself to live with a total stranger?

Susanne gestured back out to the hallway. "Let's go upstairs, shall we? See what might be Oliver's room."

They followed her up the stairs and into one of the bedrooms at the front.

Like the rest of the house it was brightly decorated and light and airy. The big bay windows gave a view out onto the street. A white painted desk was against one wall, a single bed against the other. There was a chest of drawers for Ollie's clothes and a wardrobe for anything he might want to hang up. She did her best to picture Oliver living here, and a swell of mixed emotions rushed inside her chest.

"You can bring anything you want from home," Susanne said. "If you've got your own duvets and sheets, or pictures for the walls, then you're more than welcome to have them here. Make the place your own."

"What about my puzzle trolley?" Oliver asked.

She smiled brightly. "Of course you can bring your trolley. There's plenty of space for it in here, or else you can keep it down in the common room if you prefer?"

Oliver's expression flattened at the suggestion. "Not the common room. Other people will try to touch it."

She laughed. "Okay, in your room then. We wouldn't want anyone to mess up your puzzles."

"No, that would be very bad. They can help if I'm there, though."

"Well, that sounds like a good compromise."

They went back to the ground floor again. Susanne turned to Oliver.

"Oliver, why don't you go and see Paul for a moment. Let me have a chat with Mallory?"

Ollie happily vanished into the other room to see his friend.

"How are you feeling about all of this?" Susanne asked.

"Honestly, a bit weird. A bit sad. I know it's the right thing for him, but at the same time it's hard not to feel..." she sought for the right word... "rejected."

"That's perfectly normal. Most family members feel exactly the same way. Do you have any support yourself?"

"Our parents are still around. They'll be popping in to see Ollie all the time, too."

She raised an eyebrow. "And will they be popping to see you as well?"

Mallory realised she hadn't even thought of it. Whenever her parents had come to the house, she always assumed it was for Ollie. She was in her thirties now, a detective, no less, and had never considered that she still needed the support of her parents. She was the one who did the supporting—the taking care of—not the other way around.

Susanne continued. "Take some time to think about it. I'll hold the room for Ollie until you both decide what's right. No rush. If Oliver does decide he wants to give it a go, we can do a trial run with him staying here for a week or so, see how he gets on. No pressure. If he decides it's not for him, you're not signed into any kind of contract. With these vulnerable young adults, we wouldn't force them to live in a place where they don't feel comfortable."

"Thank you, that's very kind. I think Ollie has pretty much already made up his mind, though."

To her delight, Oliver's raucous laughter came from the other room. The two women caught each other's eye and couldn't help but join in.

Chapter Twenty-One

Ryan had spent the evening with Donna. They'd gone to see a film at the cinema, but he'd struggled to concentrate on the plot, and even when they'd gone to grab some food afterwards, he'd couldn't focus on the conversation.

"Go home," Donna had told him eventually. "Or go back into the office. I know this—" She'd waved her finger around in the air in front of him.

"Know what?" he'd said.

"This distracted Ryan. I've known you long enough to not even bother to try to compete. Your body might be here, but your head and heart are clearly lost in a case."

He'd reached across the table and took her hand. "Sorry I'm such shit company. It's just I've got two bodies and absolutely no leads on who might be responsible. I'm worried there might be a third."

"You really think there might be?"

"If the killer actually is choosing his victims at random, then yes, quite possibly. I don't think he's done yet."

Donna's features had knotted together in concern. "What do you know about him? You seem sure it's a he?"

Ryan had nodded. "We have an image from a dashcam, but it's not too clear. We can see the killer is male, white, about six feet and medium build, but that's all. It doesn't exactly narrow things down. It's not the first time we potentially caught him on camera either, but the first time the footage is from too far away to get any idea if the figure was even male or female."

In the end, he'd taken Donna up on the offer and cut the meal short. An early night had meant he was able to get back into work first thing where he went back through all the information he had from both murders, scouring every detail for something he might have missed that linked the two victims.

He paused on the image of the murderer, standing on top of the bridge. Maybe they did need to put it to more use.

"I think we might need to consider a media appeal at this point," he told Mallory when she came in. "Take the image from the bridge and see if anyone recognises him."

"That picture is barely more than a blur."

"I know, but you can make out the outfit he's wearing. It might jolt someone's memory. Maybe they know of someone who they suspect of being up to no good, and seeing the image will give them the extra nudge to contact us."

Mallory agreed. "Okay, we'll get it over to the media team."

Ryan's phone rang, and he answered it. "Chase."

"It's Claire Mascall from digital forensics. We were able to get into Jillian Griffith's iPad, and we found something interesting on it. Turns out Jillian was online dating. She'd arranged to meet a man called Rupert Greenwood on the evening she went missing."

"Rupert Greenwood," Ryan said. "R.G."

"It means something to you?" Claire asked.

"Yes. She had the initials written on a calendar in her kitchen. We didn't know what they meant until now."

"Glad to have been of help. I was able to find his profile on the dating site, so I have his age, though whether he told the truth or not is questionable, plus a photograph. Unfortunately, these kinds of sites are known for their catfishing, so the accuracy of this information is questionable."

Ryan twirled a pen around on his desk. "Was there anything else on the iPad that caught your attention?"

"That was the main thing, but I'll get everything uploaded so you can take a gander at it yourself. The message thread between the two of them is there as well, but there's nothing that rings any alarm bells."

"Great. Thank you for your help."

He ended the call and then got Linda's attention from where she was sitting at her desk. "Linda, can you look into a man called Rupert Greenwood. It would seem Jillian had arranged to meet him that evening."

"Have we got any more details on him?" Linda asked. "I expect there will be more than one Rupert Greenwood in the city."

"I'll send everything over to you."

He let Linda get to work. Barely half an hour passed when she approached his desk with news.

"I think I've tracked the correct Rupert Greenwood down. I found a phone number, so I called him and asked if he knew a Jillian Griffiths. He said he knew of her, but they'd never actually met as she'd stood him up."

Could this Rupert Greenwood be their killer? It seemed unlikely. Why use your correct name on the internet if you'd planned on killing someone?

Linda continued, "He sent her a message later that evening calling her rude for standing him up, but that could just be him covering his back. Obviously, she didn't reply, but there's a good chance that's because she was already missing at this point."

"Does he have any kind of record?"

"No. He's a sixty-four-year-old plumber. Twice divorced, according to his dating profile."

Ryan sat back and let out a breath. "I think I'd like to talk to him. I could do with getting out of the office. Do you have an address for him?"

She slid a piece of paper onto Ryan's desk. "He's home right now."

"Thanks, Linda." He thought for a second. "Oh, did you tell him the reason we wanted to speak to him about Jillian?"

"No, I didn't tell him she was dead. Just that it was a police matter."

Ryan let Linda get on with other tasks.

He caught his sergeant's attention. "Feel like a drive, Mallory?"

She tossed the pen she'd been writing with onto her desk. "Yep. Let's get out of here."

THEY CAUGHT RUPERT Greenwood loading equipment into the back of his white van, both of the back doors standing open. A white van always caught Ryan's attention when there was an abduction involved. There had been one spotted not far from where Gary Carter had died, but then there were countless white vans in the city, and, despite their best efforts, they'd been unable to get the registration for the one they'd caught on camera.

Greenwood was a wide-set man with a bald head and wrinkles across the back of his neck. A gap between the bottom of his t-shirt and the top of his jeans exposed far more flesh than was necessary.

Ryan found himself thinking back to the photographs he'd seen of Jillian Griffiths—an attractive woman who'd clearly cared about appearances—and wondered what she'd seen in Rupert Greenwood. Then he remembered that she'd only ever seen pictures of him online.

"Mr Greenwood?" Ryan said to the man's back. He held up his ID for Greenwood to see as he turned around.

"Yes?"

"I'm DI Ryan Chase, and this is DS Lawson. You spoke to one of my colleagues earlier about Jillian Griffiths. I'd like to expand on that conversation, if possible."

His large forehead furrowed. "I'm just heading out to a job."

"This won't take long, and it really is important. I'm afraid I'm going to have to insist." Ryan gestured to the man's front door. "Shall we go inside."

Rupert appeared to be considering giving them an argument, but then his shoulder's dropped. "Fine. Ten minutes."

Ryan and Mallory followed him into the house. He led them into the living room and gestured for them to sit down before dropping into one of the chairs.

"What's this all about then? I really don't know what you want from me. I never even met Jillian Griffiths."

"I'm sorry to tell you that Jillian was killed yesterday morning. We believe you may be one of the last people to have had contact with her."

His jaw dropped. "Dead? How?"

Ryan filled him in on what had happened, while leaving out the part about her mutilated mouth.

"Jesus Christ." Rupert shook his head. "I thought I'd just been stood up, not that she'd been killed. I read about a woman being thrown in front of a lorry. I never imagined for one minute that it was Jillian."

"I'm sorry for your loss," Mallory said.

"I mean, it's not really my loss." He must have realised how callous he sounded as he widened his eyes and paled. "Not that I mean it badly, it's just that we'd never even met before. The other night would have been the first time. We've exchanged a handful of messages online, but that was all."

"Can you tell me where you were the night she went missing?" Ryan asked.

Rupert screwed up his face. "Well, at the pub, waiting for her, of course."

"What time were you supposed to meet?"

"Seven o'clock. I waited until eight and tried to message her on the dating app to find out where she was, but obviously she never got back to me."

Ryan considered this. The pub where she'd arranged to meet her blind date was only a fifteen-minute walk away from her house. She might have decided to leave the car at home so she could have a drink. If she was due to meet Rupert Greenwood at seven, they could assume she would have left her home sometime between six-thirty and seven. If they knew which route she would have most likely walked, they potentially had both the location and the time of her abduction.

"Is there anyone who can verify that?"

Rupert lifted his hand to rub the top of his head, and Ryan noted the slight shake to it. Was that because he was nervous? Or upset about the news of Jillian's death? He didn't seem particularly upset, and if he was nervous, what was the reason behind it? Unless there was another reason for the tremor, of course.

"The bar staff at the pub can," Rupert said. "They were sympathising with me about me being stood up. They'll remember me."

"Where did you go once you'd decided she wasn't coming?"

"I just went straight home. I was a bit pissed off, to be honest. I felt like she'd wasted my time. Obviously, I didn't know something bad had happened to her. I thought she'd just changed her mind."

Ryan had thought the same thing when he'd first seen Rupert Greenwood. There was always the possibility that she had turned up, but then decided he wasn't for her, and left again. Rupert was right—that would have been rude—but they couldn't rule it out until they knew exactly what time Jillian had been abducted.

"Is there anyone at home who can verify that?" he asked.

"No, it's just me. The neighbours might have seen me arrive back, though."

Rupert reached into his pocket and produced his phone. He checked the time, and the phone trembled in his grip. "Is this going to take much longer? I'm going to be late for a customer."

Ryan nodded at the other man's hand. "What did you do to your hand, Mr Greenwood?"

Rupert glanced at it as though something had changed. "Oh, I had a mild stroke a few years ago. I made a full recovery, with the exception of my left hand. I haven't been able to use it properly since. It's a bit of a bugger, 'cause I'm left-handed, and it does affect my work. I had to teach myself to use my right hand, which wasn't easy at my age. I've still got use of it, as you can see, but some days are better than others. I'd like to retire soon, but there's a fat chance of that happening with everything being so expensive."

"I'm sorry to hear that." Ryan turned to Mallory. "I think we have everything we need?"

She nodded and closed her notebook and slid it inside her jacket pocket.

Ryan got to his feet. "Thank you for your time, Mr Greenwood."

The three of them left the house, with Rupert locking up behind them and then going back to his vehicle.

Ryan waited until they'd got in the car, and Rupert had climbed inside his van, before he turned to his sergeant.

"What do you think?"

She twisted her lips. "Well, we need to confirm his alibi before we decide anything for sure."

Ryan played devil's advocate. "The alibi doesn't mean anything. He could have abducted Jillian, locked her in somewhere, and then driven back to the pub to create his alibi."

"That's true. If he'd found out where she lived, then he would have known what route she was taking."

"There's just one thing that makes me think he can't be our killer, not unless he has an accomplice."

Mallory narrowed her eyes. "What makes you say that?"

"His hand. His fine motor skills are no good. There's no way he could have stitched up the victims' mouths so perfectly with that hand."

"Could he be faking it? It would be a good way to throw us off the scent?"

"We can check medical records, but I don't think so. There's something else, too. Do you remember the dashcam footage of the killer on the bridge?

Mallory nodded. "Of course."

"The person the camera caught was tall and of a leaner build. Rupert Greenwood has a much wider gut. His silhouette would be more of a barrel shape."

"You're right. So unless he's working with someone, he's not our man."

Ryan thought out loud. "Does he have any connection with the wood fibres? What about his job as a plumber? Is that something he'd ever come into contact with?"

"Not that I'm aware of. I'm not exactly an expert in the area, though."

"No. I wonder if Grewal has made any progress tracking down an expert." He made a mental note to chase him up when they got back to the office.

"Jillian hadn't told her family that she was online dating," Mallory said, sitting back and yanking the seatbelt across her chest.

"Perhaps she thought they'd disapprove?"

"Maybe, but isn't that how everyone meets these days?"

Ryan rolled his eyes. "God, I hope not. What's wrong with getting drunk in a bar and picking someone up like we did in the good old days?"

"I'm sure that still happens, but I doubt a woman of Jillian's age would have done much hanging out in bars. That's a young person's game."

"I bet Jillian would have strung you up for saying that," he said with a rueful smile. "Sixty is no age at all."

Chapter Twenty-Two

Olwen pulled into the car park for the residential home. She climbed out of the car and wrapped her coat tightly around her body.

The air held a chill today, the leaves on the trees losing their green chlorophyll to reveal the reds and browns beneath. Soon they would be littering the ground, and winter would well and truly be here.

She hit the buzzer to be allowed entry into the building. Another buzzer sounded somewhere inside, releasing the door, and she opened it and stepped inside. The home was always several degrees hotter than any normal place would be kept at—the residents tended to feel the cold—and she quickly found herself stripping off her layers again.

Olwen signed in at the visitor's book and flashed a quick smile at one of the carers behind the reception desk.

She went to her father's room, lightly knocked on the door, and entered.

He was sitting in his high-backed chair at the window that looked onto the garden.

She forced her tone to be bright. "Hi, Dad. How are you today?"

He turned his head at the sound of her voice. "I thought you were bringing my lunch?"

Olwen found herself glancing back at the door, as though the meal might have followed her in. "Umm, I don't think it's quite lunchtime yet."

"Isn't it?"

"No, but if you're hungry, I'll have a word with one of the carers. Haven't you got any of those biscuits left that I brought you the other day? The shortbread ones with the chocolate chips? You can't have eaten them all already?"

She busied herself by checking the cupboard where he kept all his bits and pieces. Sure enough, the packet of shortbread was still in there, unopened. She took them out and tore the packet so she could hand one to him.

He took the biscuit and bit into it, his gaze drifting back to the window.

Olwen dragged up another chair so she could sit next to him.

She took the hand that wasn't occupied with the shortbread. His skin was so thin now, like crepe paper, and the purple and blue veins bulged beneath it. He'd always been such a strong man, and it broke her heart to see him like this. Maybe he'd never been the most loving of fathers; she couldn't remember him ever saying that he loved her, or even giving her a hug, but things had been different back then. To be fair, she wasn't even sure she could remember her mother being particularly affectionate when she'd been little either. She'd grown up with the influence of 'you need to be strong, to be tough, to make it in the world', and she'd done her best to emulate that. Nowadays, children were taught that it was okay to show their feelings and talk about what was upsetting them.

She wondered if that was why she was still single. She'd been so busy being strong that she'd never dared to truly open her heart to anyone. She'd always felt the need to protect herself, emotionally. But then it wasn't as though the men she'd met had made her feel any differently. All they'd done was confirm that protecting her softer insides was a good idea.

"Dad," she started hesitantly. "Do you remember when we lived on Ellebie Street?"

She highly doubted he would have any clue what she was talking about. She wasn't really expecting a response. She just wanted to have someone to talk to—especially someone who'd been there at the time.

Her father's watery blue eyes flickered over to hers. Something about the look in them told her he remembered. It was often the case with Alzheimer's patients that they could remember something that had happened to them when they were younger, thinking they were still living in that time, rather than being able to recall what they'd had for breakfast that morning.

"I remember that house," he said.

Her heart picked up its beat.

"Do you remember the property next door that you and Mum bought? The one that was used to house the foster kids?"

His fingers tightened around hers. "Elanor?"

"No, Dad. It's me, Olwen. Your daughter, remember?"

"We can't talk about that, Elanor. You know we can't. Someone might hear."

Spikes of alarm went through her. What was he talking about?

"Hear what? Why can't you talk about it?"

He yanked his hand out of her grip. "Stop it! Why are you doing this?"

She wanted to cry. "I'm not doing anything, Dad. I only wanted to ask you about when I was growing up. I just wanted to talk to you, that's all. I didn't mean to upset you."

He reached out and swiped everything off the little roller table: his glass of water, the box of tissues, the remote control for the television, though he rarely used it. The items crashed to the floor, the glass shattering and water flying everywhere.

Olwen jumped to her feet. "Dad!"

He clutched his hands to his head, wrenching at the small amount of hair he had left. The sound peeling from his lips wrought her heart, and her hands fluttered towards him. She was desperate to do something to help but frightened of making things worse. Shards of glass littered the floor, and she was worried he'd cut himself if he tried to get up.

The door opened, and one of the nurse's heads popped in. "Everything okay?"

Olwen shook her head, the tears that had been welling now spilling down her cheeks. "No, I upset him. I'm sorry. I don't know what I said."

The nurse came fully into the room. "It's okay. It's not your fault."

"Be careful," Olwen said. "There's glass all over the floor."

"Is everything all right, Mr Morgan?" The nurse raised her voice slightly. "What can I do to help?"

He raised a shaking hand. "Get her out of here. I don't want her here."

Olwen placed her hand to her mouth and gulped back a sob.

The nurse crouched at his side. "That's Olwen, Mr Morgan. That's your daughter."

"I don't want her here!" he insisted.

The nurse glanced up at her, her eyes swimming with an apology. "Perhaps it's best if he gets some rest."

Olwen pressed her lips together and nodded. "It's okay, I'll go."

She threw a final glance towards her father then slipped out of the room. She felt embarrassed and rejected and unloved. Though she told herself it was the disease and not really him who had shouted at her to leave, it had still upset her. What if he never wanted to see her again and that had been the last conversation she ever had with him?

What was it that had set him off so badly? Had it been the mention of the house or that he'd thought she was her mother?

Olwen put her head down, hiding in the collar of her coat in the hope no one else in the home would see how upset she was and ask her if she was okay. She was sure even one kind word from a stranger would find her inconsolable. She moved at a fast walk, just shy of breaking into a run, and hit the button beside the doors to unlock them so she could make her escape. She ran out into the car park, fumbled for her keys in her bag, and found them. The car's headlights flashed as she pressed the correct button on the fob, and she opened the driver's door and threw herself inside.

It was only when she'd pulled the door shut behind her again that she gave in to her tears. They started as a trickle then descended into full-blown sobbing, her hands covering her face, her shoulders shaking. What was so wrong with her that nobody loved her? Anyone who'd ever come into her life had left again.

Now she had this horrible, gnawing sensation inside her that something terrible had happened back at that house. Something that her father had known about and had been kept a secret from her. Had she blocked something out? When she tried to think back to those days, she was only rewarded with snapshots of that time. Only brief moments appeared clear in her memory. That was normal, though, wasn't it? Who could remember clearly events from thirty years ago?

Olwen thought about Helen's suggestion to speak to her aunt. It had been a while since they'd had any contact, but surely her Aunt Millicent wouldn't mind hearing from her only niece?

Chapter Twenty-Three

There had been a development. Gary Carter's car had been found dumped in a field in the countryside outside of Winford.

Ryan drove to the location of the abandoned vehicle, taking one of his constables with him. Uniformed police were already on scene, creating a cordon around the car. It would be towed so that forensics could investigate in more detail, but for the moment, they needed to work with the vehicle in situ.

The vehicle was a light-grey Honda CR-V, an older model, obscured from the road by the hedgerow. Mud had been churned up behind the wheels. Deep ruts in the soft ground created a track from the gate that opened onto the road to the position of the car.

"The farmer who owns the field reported it," DC Dev Patel said. "The field is arable and has only been used to grow grass, so he hasn't had any reason to come in here until now. He said it was only luck that he found it in the first place while he was taking a walk around the land."

The driver's door stood open by a couple of inches, as though whoever had dumped it had been in a rush and had forgotten to shut it properly.

"Did the farmer touch the vehicle at all?" Ryan asked.

"No, he said he called it in straight away. Didn't touch anything."

"Good."

"The keys are in the ignition," Dev said, peering through the window.

"Whoever dumped it clearly didn't care if someone stole it then." Ryan moved around the outside of the car. "Maybe it would have even done the killer a favour if someone had pinched it. Helped to cover his tracks."

Dev pulled on a pair of gloves from his pocket and opened the door fully.

"Are there any signs of violence?" Ryan asked.

Dev leaned into the car. "No obvious ones, but forensics will be able to get a better look once it's been towed."

Ryan put on his own gloves then opened the passenger door. He wasn't one hundred percent sure what they were going to find. It was unlikely the killer would have left something with his name on it in the car, but stranger things had happened.

He did spot something in the passenger footwell.

"Look." He picked up the carrier bag and checked inside. "It's the shopping Gary did when we caught him on CCTV."

"We know he got back in his car," Dev said, "but he didn't make it home. If he made it back to his car, why did he stop to give the killer the opportunity to attack him?"

"Maybe the killer flagged him down somewhere along the country roads and attacked him then. Then he put Gary into his own car and drove this one into the field and left it."

Dev seemed to muse on this for a moment. "The question is, did the killer intentionally stop Gary? If so, he must have known the route Gary drove home from work."

A bulb illuminated in Ryan's head. "If that's the case, then whoever killed him already knew the victim's routine, which meant they took time to follow him. We need to check CCTV around his home and workplace, and anywhere else he might have gone, during the days and even weeks before his death. Find out if there's someone who shows up repeatedly who can't be accounted for. There's a chance we've caught the perpetrator on camera somewhere."

It was going to mean a lot of hours sitting in front of computer screens, scrolling through footage, but that just came with the job.

Ryan and Dev continued their search of the vehicle, checking in the boot, tugging up the mats in the footwells, moving the seats. Forensics would do a far more thorough job, taking samples from both the inside and outside of the car. Dirt or soil from a different area might be caught in the hubcaps and give them a clue as to where the car had been before it ended up in the field.

Ryan imagined Gary on his way home from his nightshift at work, his shopping in the footwell, most likely tired and looking forward to a meal and a good sleep. What reason would he have to stop for someone?

"He's getting his victim's attention somehow," Ryan said as he slammed the boot shut. "Convincing them to stop."

"Jillian Griffiths was on foot," Dev pointed out.

Ryan thought for a moment. "Is it possible the killer was known to both the victims?"

"Known how?"

"I'm not sure, but who would you be more likely to go with or stop for? A stranger or someone you knew?"

"Someone I knew," Dev said.

"Exactly. Maybe they went with the killer willingly, or at least willingly stopped and spoke with them. Perhaps that was even how he was able to get the Rohypnol in their system?"

Dev straightened from the vehicle and removed his gloves. "But who could be linking them together? We haven't found any connections between the two victims yet."

Ryan glanced out across the patchwork of brown and green fields. "Just because we haven't found it yet, doesn't mean there isn't one. We just need to figure it out."

Chapter Twenty-Four

The visit with her father had stirred up more questions than it had answered. Olwen was filled with the certainty that what Andy and the others had said about the foster home was correct. She hated the possibility that her parents had known the children in the home were being abused by someone and yet had done nothing to stop it. Or maybe they had done something and that was why they'd shut the home down in the first place. But why wouldn't they have just fired whoever was responsible instead?

Olwen remembered her aunt's disapproval of the place.

Had Aunt Millicent felt that way because she'd been aware of what was going on there?

Olwen knew she wasn't going to get any rest until she found out exactly what had happened. Perhaps she'd be better off getting in touch with Andy and the others and asking them directly, but the shame of it was overwhelming. It made her feel as though she was responsible somehow, even though she'd only been a child herself back then.

Instead, she'd decided to drop her aunt a message, asking her if she wanted to meet for coffee sometime. Aunt Millie had been delighted to hear from her, and they'd arranged to meet the very same day.

Olwen arrived at the coffee shop early, already anxious. Though she wanted the truth, a part of her was worried about what she'd find out. Already, her memories of the past had been reshaped. That her parents had been harbouring some terrible secret all these years changed how she saw them. It wasn't that she thought they'd been involved directly, but had they been complicit in covering up for someone else? Had they known one of their staff had been abusing the kids, and they'd done what they needed to cover it up? In doing so, they'd have allowed that person to walk away, unpunished. The perpetrator might have even gone straight into another job involving children, and the cycle of abuse would have started all over again.

She'd expected to be the first to arrive, but the back of a familiar head caught her attention. Her aunt was already sitting at one of the tables, facing away from the door.

Olwen gripped the strap of her handbag tighter and crossed the busy café.

"Aunt Milly?"

The last time she'd seen her aunt had been at her mother's funeral, and even then, she'd seemed distant. What was it about their family? Why did everyone have this need to keep each other at arm's length?

The older woman turned in her chair, clocked Olwen standing there, and then got to her feet.

"Olwen!"

To Olwen's surprise, Millicent enveloped Olwen in a hug. Olwen froze for a split second, and then hugged her back. The physical contact took her by surprise. When was the last time she hugged her aunt?

They broke apart, though Aunt Milly kept her hands on Olwen's shoulders so she could get a better view of her niece.

"You look tired."

Olwen risked a smile. "Thanks, Aunt Milly. You're looking well, too."

"Don't be so sensitive. I'm only saying it 'cause I care."

You haven't cared enough to see me since Mum's funeral. She kept her words to herself. It wasn't as though she'd made the effort either. Millicent had never hidden her feelings about Olwen's father from any of them, and there had always been a kind of unspoken agreement that while he was still around, Milly wouldn't be. Olwen knew it had been a cause of great heartache for her mother, having to make that choice between her sister or her husband, but neither of them would agree to any kind of truce, so Milly had just stayed away.

It had been such a waste, in Olwen's opinion. She would have loved to have had a sibling instead of being an only child. She'd watched friends at school with older or younger brothers and sisters. They'd been sources of great irritation, she was sure, but also companionship. Olwen had spent most of her childhood alone, and it wasn't until the foster home opened that she finally felt like she understood what it was to have a family. They might have been troublemakers in everyone else's minds, but they'd been her friends.

So why had she never stayed in touch with them? Why had they moved, and she hadn't kicked up a fuss or fought to see any of them?

A short, girthy waitress in her sixties came around, giving them both a warm smile. "What can I get you?"

"Just a white coffee for me," Olwen said.

Millicent glanced up at the waitress. "I'll take a pot of tea."

The waitress scribbled the order in her notepad. "I'll be back with your drinks in a tick."

"So, how have you been?" Olwen asked.

"Oh, you know...so-so. My hip's been playing up, and I've got arthritis in my fingers now, but I'm sure you didn't get in touch to hear about all my issues."

The waitress returned with their drinks, and the two women fell silent while she set them on the table. They both thanked her, and she left, and they continued their conversation as though she'd never been there.

Olwen pressed her lips together and shook her head. "No, I didn't. I wanted to talk to you about something."

"Something to do with your father?"

Olwen straightened. "How did you know?"

"Lucky guess."

Olwen took a breath. "I went to see him the other day—"

Aunt Milly interrupted her. "He's still alive then?"

The coldness in her aunt's voice shocked her. "Yes, of course. I would have told you if he'd passed."

"I thought that might be the reason you'd asked to meet. You haven't been in touch in a long time."

So that was the reason her aunt had been so enthusiastic about the meeting. She'd thought Olwen was going to tell her that her father was dead. A surge of an emotion she couldn't quite decipher rose inside her.

"Well, it wasn't, and neither have you. The phone goes both ways, you know."

Millicent sniffed. "It's not like I have much other family. I thought you were supposed to be taking care of me by now."

"You're only in your early sixties, Aunt Milly. It's not like you're an old lady."

She sighed and pushed back her hair. "I feel like it some days. So how *is* your father?"

"He's not good. Alzheimer's. He started going downhill the moment Mum died."

"Those two always had an unhealthy relationship. I said it from the start. More like they were co-dependent on each other than anything else. They never let anyone else in, not even their own daughter."

Milly was right. Olwen had always felt like she'd come second best to her parents' relationship. A lot of people would argue that she'd been lucky to have parents who'd had such a close relationship, but sometimes she imagined it was like being a sibling to twins who had their own secret language. She always felt like she was on the outside of things.

"He just couldn't cope without her," Olwen said, twisting her coffee cup between her hands, allowing the heat to seep through her palms, hoping it would warm the rest of her body.

Could it get as deep as her heart?

Millicent raised her eyebrows. "She could have coped without him, though, but he never gave her the chance."

Olwen wasn't completely sure what that meant, and she didn't want to ask. There was something else she needed to question her aunt about.

"Do you remember when we lived on Ellebie Street, and my parents bought that house next door."

That pinch of disapproval crossed Milly's face again. "Yes, of course. I warned them it was a bad idea."

"Why was it a bad idea?"

"Because they had you. They should have been protecting you, not exposing you to the sorts of kids that place attracted."

"Sorts of kids? What do you mean by that?"

"You know what I mean. Troublemakers. No one in the area wanted that place opened. It was only because the council were desperate for more foster places that they even got permission. It was messed up, the way your parents handled it. Foster homes are supposed to be places kids are cared for and nurtured and shown how to live normal, family lives. That house was more like a slum for wayward teens. Your parents never showed those children a moment of attention—they just paid other random people to do it. It's not as though your parents were the nurturing kind in the first place. They didn't even know how to show love and affection to their only child, so God knows how they were ever supposed to be a good influence on those foster kids. I bet neither of your parents would have even been able to tell you one of the teenagers' names."

She didn't reply, allowing her aunt's words to sink in. She was completely right.

"They didn't cause much trouble, though, did they? The foster kids, I mean."

Her lips tightened. "There were...rumours. Accusations."

"Accusations of what?"

"All the usual stuff. Drinking, drugs, stealing, underage sex..."

Her gaze shifted, and Olwen could tell there was more.

"Is that why they shut the place down?"

Millicent stared at her. "Do you really not remember?"

Olwen swallowed hard. "Are—are you talking about there being abuse at the home?"

"It was never proven, but there were rumours."

"Abuse by the staff?"

Aunt Milly glanced away. "No one was ever held to account, but the council stepped in and shut the place down. That was when you and your parents moved."

"Didn't Mum ever say anything to you about it?" Olwen asked.

"God, no. She wouldn't talk about it at all. I remember trying to talk to her about the move and what led up to it, and she said that it was spiteful neighbours who didn't want the home open who were spreading rumours about the place."

"Did you believe her?"

Aunt Milly shrugged. "It did make sense. No one wanted the home on their street. Those kids *were* troublemakers."

Olwen's defensiveness rose inside her on behalf of the others. "They weren't troublemakers. They were children who'd been let down by the adults in their lives. They had broken home lives or abusive parents or lived in such poverty that they'd been forced to shoplift in order to eat."

Her aunt snorted softly. "Plenty of people come from those kinds of backgrounds and don't resort to stealing and drinking and taking drugs. It's easy to make excuses for people."

"Some of them were barely teenagers—fourteen years old. How can you write someone off at that age? They had their whole lives ahead of them."

She couldn't help thinking of poor Philip, the kid who'd decided suicide was a better option than continuing with his life. Her heart seemed to stutter, and she struggled to take her next breath. How much had living in the foster home contributed to him making that choice? If he'd been placed in a normal family home, with two adults who had loved and nurtured him, would he still be alive today?

Had, even if it was indirectly, her parents contributed to Philip's death by allowing abuse to carry on right under their noses?

She remembered the boy with the spikey black hair. Had she even had a bit of a crush on him back then? He hadn't been one of the loud ones, hadn't put his fist through a wall like Wesley had, or been found doing weird stuff like Samuel. He'd been a joker, but there had always been a measure of pain in his eyes. It was as though he'd used his pranks and jokes to cover up whatever torment he was going through inside.

Milly sighed and shook her head. "You're looking at this from the point of view of a child. You don't remember the number of times the police were called because a fight had broken out between the residents, or when the place was raided because there was a report of one of the boys selling drugs out of his room."

It was true. Olwen didn't really remember much of the bad stuff. Sure, she remembered getting into a bit of trouble with them herself—drinking properly for the first time, smoking, even sneaking out of her bedroom when her parents thought she was asleep so she could go and hang out with them all—but nothing bad had ever happened, had it? It had just been the normal teenager stuff that most kids go through.

"Maybe you're right."

"Of course I am," her aunt reassured her. Milly leaned across the table and squeezed Olwen's hand. "Now, how about we change the subject, okay? I'm sure there are better things we could talk about. Did I tell you I have a man now? He's younger than me, so I guess you could call me a bit of a cougar."

Olwen allowed Millicent to steer the conversation away from the foster home, though every word still lingered in the back of her mind. She didn't think she was any clearer about what had happened back then than she was before. All anyone kept telling her was that those kids had been trouble. Yes, maybe they had been, but that didn't explain her father's reaction when she'd tried to talk about it. It didn't explain why one of the foster kids had ended up killing himself. Had there really been abuse at the home? Or had it been a cruel rumour started by the neighbours to get the place shut down?

Deep down, she knew she had to get in touch with Andy again. He would tell her the truth, wouldn't he? She'd walked out on him, and he might not even want to see her again, but if she didn't ask, she'd never know.

It occurred to her that even he might not tell her the whole truth. What if Andy was the one with some kind of vendetta against her family and he was using her as a way of venting it? He could have even been the one to start the rumours, for all she knew.

Who could she trust?

Chapter Twenty-Five

After work, Mallory stopped at her local corner shop to pick up some groceries for the house before heading home. She knew there wouldn't be enough milk for the morning, otherwise, and they were down to the final crusts of bread in the bread bin. Finding the time to get a big food shop done was always difficult, and she tended to have to pick up meals every couple of days to keep them going instead. She smiled at the man behind the counter, a moment of recognition at the number of times she used the shop passing between them.

She knew where everything was on the shelves, so it only took her a matter of minutes to chuck what she needed into a basket and then carry it over to pay.

"You had a good day?" the man behind the counter asked her.

She gave him a polite smile. "Not too bad. You?"

"Nothing too exciting ever happens working here."

She didn't know what to say to that but decided she wouldn't give him the rundown of how she'd spent her day trying to track down a killer who liked to cut out tongues, sew up mouths, and then throw their victims in front of vehicles.

She packed up her items of shopping in a foldup canvas bag she always kept in her coat pocket and thanked him again and stepped back out onto the pavement to return to her car.

All the parking spaces had been taken when she'd arrived—though annoyingly one was now free directly in front of the shop—so she'd had to park a short way down the road. She shivered at the chill in the air, made a mental note to dig out her gloves, and put her head down to walk back to the car.

A figure stepped out in front of her.

Mallory drew to a halt to prevent walking straight into them. Almost instantly, she realised it was a man. A split second later, her heart leapt as his identity hit her.

"Daniel? What the fuck are you doing here?"

She should turn around and run straight back to the convenience shop. The man behind the counter would help her. But she hated having to run from one man to the aid of another. She was a strong woman. A police detective. She resented being made to feel this way.

"I haven't been able to stop thinking about you."

Mallory squared her shoulders. "I should arrest you right now for breaking your restraining order. You're not allowed to come within one hundred feet of me."

Why wasn't she arresting him? She should, but she couldn't seem to get her body to respond to her brain. Her feet had rooted into the pavement. Blood rushed through her ears, so loud it made all the other noises of the city seem distant. Where was everyone? Why was the street suddenly deserted?

A part of her had always known this day would come. Even though she told herself that he had a restraining order, she worked for the police. She knew if an abusive partner really wanted to harm a woman, then it didn't mean a thing. Not that she'd ever thought of Daniel as being her partner. They'd had a few dates, that was all. It had never been serious—at least, not in her mind. Daniel had clearly felt differently.

He'd never actually cared for her. Maybe he told himself it was love, but all he really wanted was to control her. He hadn't liked her rejection of him and was punishing her for it.

She'd hoped Ryan coming to her rescue last time would have been enough to see him off, but it clearly hadn't. She despised needing to rely on a man to 'save' her. It wasn't who she was at all. But men like Daniel often only listened to other men.

Her mind whirred, trying to predict what was going to happen. If he walked away now, he must know that she'd have him arrested for breaking the restraining order. Which meant he didn't plan on walking away—at least not without finishing things with her first.

"I'm nowhere near your house," he said. "It's not my fault if we happen to be on the same street, is it?"

"You've orchestrated this. I know you have."

He angled his jaw, his eyes glinting in the streetlight. "Prove it?"

She ground her molars. "If you haven't planned this, you should keep walking. You're not supposed to be communicating with me either."

"Maybe you should be the one to keep walking?" he challenged.

"Fine."

She forced her feet to respond, stepping to one side to get past him. Deep down, she'd known he was just playing with her. Instead of letting her pass, he stepped to one side as well, blocking her way. She tried to move the other way, and he did the same.

He laughed, but the sound was cold. "Oops."

"Please, Daniel…"

She cringed at the begging, whining tone of her voice, but she was terrified. He was going to kill her; she had no doubt. He hadn't managed it last time because of Ryan, but then Ryan had humiliated him, and now he was back to punish her for it.

"Where's your new boyfriend today then, huh? Not here to save you?"

"He's not my boyfriend. He's my boss."

Why was she even trying to justify things to him?

"Your boss? I should have known you'd fuck your way to the top."

Her temper snapped. That was so fucking unfair, it was ludicrous. She was practically a born-again virgin with the amount of action she got. Her last attempt at a relationship had been with Daniel, and she could barely remember who she'd been with before then. Her life had always been about taking care of other people—from her brother to her parents, to all the civilians she helped through her work.

Mallory opened and closed her fists. "Fuck you, Daniel."

He scoffed. "Bet you'd like to. Fucking prick tease."

She trembled all over, but it was partly down to anger now, as well as fear. What was her best option? Try to get past him and keep going? Turn around and run the other way? Would he catch her?

She wished someone would drive or walk by. Bristol was never this quiet. It was as though the whole city had conspired to give Daniel his moment.

She could scream for help. Someone might hear her. But if she did that, he'd do whatever it took to shut her up again, including killing her. She didn't deserve for her life to end like this. Not at the hands of this fucking prick.

Mallory set her jaw and locked her eyes on him. She could almost feel the hatred radiating out of her. She built on that rage, stoking it, nurturing it. Daniel might be here to punish her, but she wasn't going to go down without a fight.

Keeping her shoulders back, she stepped forwards, closing the gap between them. "I'm a prick tease, huh? Isn't that just the name men give to women who aren't interested in them?"

"No, you knew exactly what you were doing. It was all just a game for you. Messing me around, leading me on."

"Maybe you're right." She allowed the slightest tweak to affect the corners of her mouth. "Perhaps I was just fighting my feelings."

He angled his head. "You were."

She could almost see his ears prick up.

She shrugged. "I was worried about how it would work with my brother, but he's moving out now."

He was suspicious of her, but his own huge ego allowed him to think there might actually be some truth in her words.

"He is?"

"Yeah, so things will be different. I don't want us to fight."

She took another step closer.

He clearly didn't know how to take her change in attitude. For once, it looked as though he was the one who was considering bolting.

Mallory put down her shopping and reached out, casually lacing her hands around the back of his neck, as though she might be thinking about kissing him. His expression morphed into one of pure triumph.

She tightened her fingers on his neck for a fraction of a second and then clenched her teeth and lifted her knee, hard and fast. Her kneecap made direct contact with his balls, and his eyes widened in shock and disbelief that she'd dare do this to him. Time seemed to freeze, but then he wheezed in a breath. She darted out of the way as he folded in two, his hands clutched between his legs.

"You fucking bitch," he managed between breaths, his voice thin and reedy. "I'll fucking kill you for this."

He would as well. She believed him one hundred percent.

Leaving her shopping sitting on the pavement beside him, she ran past him and got to her car. She locked the doors behind her. Her heart pounded, and she felt sick from the adrenaline. She forced herself to think. She needed to have him arrested for breaking his restraining order, though she doubted anything would come of it.

Mallory put in the call.

Chapter Twenty-Six

The following morning, Mallory got into work an hour earlier than necessary. She'd barely slept all night and had just lain in bed, wide awake, listening out for every creak or click that might signal someone coming into the house. No matter how much she told herself it couldn't be Daniel, because he'd been taken into custody for breaking the restraining order, her imagination kept conjuring up him breaking in.

"You didn't need to come in today, Mallory," Ryan said when he spotted her already at her desk.

She nursed a coffee, knowing it wouldn't be her only one today.

"Yes, I did. I couldn't just sit at home, worrying. That would have been the worst thing to do. Oliver is out anyway and is planning his move into the other house. Being on my own all that time would have been the worst. I'm needed here where I can at least be useful."

"Even so, if you need a break, take one, okay? You don't need to tough everything out."

"I'm not, I promise. Just let me work."

He let out a sigh. "Of course. It's not like we don't need you. It's been days, and we're still no closer in finding out who could have killed Gary Carter and Jillian Griffiths. The only thing we've got connecting them is a couple of damned wood fibres, and they could have come from anywhere."

Dev caught their attention, striding across the office towards Mallory's desk. His expression was grim, but there was also a spark of excitement in his dark eyes. "A call just came in. There's been another murder."

"Same MO?" Ryan asked.

"Yep. Lips are sewn shut. I assume we'll find her tongue will be missing, too, once we've had the post-mortem done."

Ryan's fist smacked down on the desk. "Shit."

A third murder.

Another woman.

Mallory would never have said it out loud, but she was glad for the distraction. A busy crime scene meant lots of people and, right now, she felt safer surrounded by people than alone, even if there was a body involved.

Ryan pursed his lips. "Three victims. Looks like we officially have a serial killer on our hands. How was she killed?"

"Pushed out in front of a bus on the main road," Dev said. "It was doing forty miles an hour. She was killed instantly."

"A bus? There must have been plenty of witnesses then?" Ryan said.

Dev shook his head. "Unfortunately not. The driver had only just started his shift and had left the depot. The bus was empty. According to the driver, she came out of nowhere."

"Any ID on the victim?" Mallory asked.

"Not yet."

Mallory looked to her boss. "This is someone who wants to be seen. The way they're killing their victims, the mutilations beforehand, and then the public killings, it all screams that the killer is trying to send someone a message. My money would be on some kind of gang killings, if it wasn't for the victims themselves. Nothing about them says gang to me, though maybe we'll learn something new when we get the third victim's ID."

Ryan nodded his agreement. "Guess we'd better get down to the scene."

Chapter Twenty-Seven

The area of the incident was busy with emergency vehicles, red and blue lights sweeping across the still early morning sky. A couple of ambulances, one for the deceased, and another for the bus driver, waited nearby.

The blue double-decker bus sat in the middle of the road, at an angle across two lanes, where the driver had clearly tried to swerve to avoid the victim but had failed. In front of the bus, dark splashes of blood glinted on the tarmac. Streaks of skid marks lined the road behind the vehicle.

The buzz of police officers talking to one another and the crackle of a radio filled the air. Scenes of crime officers in white protective gear placed markers around the bus and the victim. A privacy tent had been erected to keep away spying eyes and anyone with a phone camera who thought it was fun to film tragedies and post them on social media sites.

A police sergeant who didn't look to be far out of his twenties approached the new arrivals, his face lit up with excitement. He had a certain swagger to his walk, his shoulders back, arms swinging.

"Detectives," he greeted Ryan and Mallory, "I'm Sergeant Gregory. I can't believe I've come to the scene of another one of those sewn-mouth killings. We thought it was just a regular RTA when it was called in. Wait till the boys hear about this."

Ryan took an instant disliking to him. "It's not a freakshow, Sergeant."

His shoulders dropped, and his gaze darted away. "No, of course not. That's not what I meant."

Ryan didn't wait for any further explanation. "Want to give me the rundown on what we know so far?"

"Yeah, sure. The paramedics did their best, but she was already dead when they arrived. It was a shock to them, too. They thought they were just dealing with an accident, but then they saw her mouth."

"Any idea who she is yet?" Ryan asked.

"Not yet. She doesn't have any belongings with her, no ID on her person. She's in her sixties, at a guess, is slender, in dark-blue leggings and a zip-up hoody in light pink. She was wearing trainers, though one fell off when she was hit by the bus.

Ryan glanced to Mallory. "A jogger, perhaps?"

She shrugged. "Possibly, though some people just like to wear workout gear because it's comfortable."

"True. Either way, she wasn't out jogging with her tongue cut out and lips sewn together."

He took a moment to absorb the surrounding area.

Four lanes of traffic ran in opposite directions, though the two heading into the city were closed. Uniformed police officers redirected the traffic which was already built up because of the road closure.

"The victim fell into the road from this side," the sergeant told them.

A low concrete wall separated the road from the grassy reserve that rose upwards at a slope. Bushes and trees topped the bank.

"Could she have been pushed from the top?" Mallory asked. "It's steep. If she was on her feet, and given a shove, she might not have been able to stop herself. She could have hit the wall and tipped right over in front of the oncoming bus."

Ryan nodded. From the position of the victim, it seemed like a reasonable guess.

"What's beyond the bank?" he asked, jerking his chin towards the slope.

"A small park," Sergeant Gregory said.

Ryan left the road and climbed up the steep grassy knoll. By the time he reached the top, his thighs burned, and he heaved for breath. He really needed to make time for some gym sessions, he reminded himself. He wasn't thirty anymore.

He paused to take in what lay ahead. Beyond the line of trees was fencing, and beyond that, the flatter and more neatly manicured space of the park—though it was a stretch to call it that really. The space didn't contain any swings for children but was just a patch of grass and trees, with a couple of paths and cycle lanes running through it. Had someone skirted the edge of the fencing to bring the victim to this point and then pushed her out into the road?

He turned and headed back down the bank, having to lean back to prevent his momentum forcing his pace into a run. He could see how the victim might have lost the ability to stop herself falling, especially if she was drugged and injured.

Ryan joined the others back on the road. "We'll need to get SOCO up there," he said. "Make sure the area is cordoned off, too."

"I'll get that done." Sergeant Gregory left them to speak to his uniformed officers.

Ryan glanced back towards the bus.

"Does the killer have some kind of vendetta against people who drive modes of public transport," Ryan wondered out loud, "or are they just being used as a convenient way of killing someone?"

Mallory pursed her lips. "Well, the drivers of the vehicles aren't the ones being killed, so my guess is the latter."

He put his hands on his hips and nodded slowly. "True. The killer doesn't mind torturing their victim but doesn't want to get their hands so dirty that they have to kill the victim themselves. They'd rather let a train or a lorry or a bus do that."

"It's removed," Mallory said. "Detached."

Ryan considered this for a moment. "Maybe they don't want to think of themselves as a murderer. Are they giving the victim the chance to live? Or at least kidding themselves that they are?"

The most recent victim could have stopped herself from ending up in the road.

Gary Carter could have got up from the track.

Could Jillian Griffiths have somehow stopped herself from falling from the bridge?

Ryan wondered if they were onto something. "None of them were tied up. Maybe the killer believed he was giving them the opportunity to run."

Mallory chuffed a small laugh. "A mutilator with a conscience. And what kind of life would they have gone on to lead with no tongue if they had survived?"

"Maybe that was part of the punishment?"

The sergeant approached again. "I just got a call. Looks like we've got an ID on the victim already. Her name is Victoria Fletcher. She was sixty-seven years old. Her husband reported her missing last night when she didn't come home after she'd attended a Pilates class at seven in the evening. He was understandably worried, called around all her friends, drove around himself to try and find her, then he called us. Misper were able to match his description of what she was wearing, and then a photograph we sent them."

"A Pilates class," Mallory said. "I guess that explains the outfit."

It was good that they'd got an ID so quickly, but Ryan couldn't help but be angry at himself for allowing the perpetrator to kill again. He'd let this poor woman's family down, and now they were going to have to figure out how to live, knowing someone had murdered their loved one.

Ryan clenched his jaw and shook his head at himself. "We have three murders now, all committed by the same perpetrator. Something is connecting the victims."

"I don't think we can ignore that each of the victims have been of a similar age," Mallory said. "There must be a reason behind it. It can't just be that the killer doesn't like people in their later stage of life."

Ryan sucked air over his teeth. "The sewn mouths. The removed tongue. Did each of the victims know something?"

He addressed the sergeant once more. "What else do we know about Victoria Fletcher?"

"Not much just yet. She worked as a social worker but retired at the age of fifty-five. Two grown-up children, four grandchildren. Married for more than forty years."

Ryan shook his head. "A married, retired grandmother? Why the hell would someone want to kill a person like that?"

Mallory frowned. "Could her career have something to do with why she's been killed? Social workers come up against conflict all the time. I imagine she'd have dealt with some tough cases in her past."

Ryan considered this for a moment. "The other two didn't have that kind of job role, though."

"Not recently," Mallory said. "But how far back have we checked?"

"Good point. We've looked at everything in the victims' presents to try and find a connection, but there isn't one. Maybe now it's time to delve a bit deeper into their pasts."

"How far back should we go?"

"As far as we need to."

Ryan's phone rang, and he took it from his pocket and checked the screen. He lifted the phone slightly as a way of indicating that he needed to take the call and then stepped away from everyone for some privacy.

"Chase," he answered.

It was one of the arresting officers who'd dealt with Daniel Williamson last night.

"I thought the news would be better coming from you," the officer told him.

Ryan listened while his colleague explained what was happening. His heart sank, and he glanced over to where Mallory was still talking with the sergeant.

This wasn't going to go down well.

Chapter Twenty-Eight

Olwen's stomach knotted as she waited for Andy. Her thoughts had been a torrent, like muddy water in a storm drain, ever since they'd last met.

She'd called him yesterday and convinced him to meet her for coffee before she started work. He'd seemed surprised at the urgency in her tone about wanting to meet sooner rather than later.

They'd agreed on a takeout place at the corner of the park—one of those mobile coffee vendors serving out of a cute little wagon. Though it was late October, the morning was bright, the threat of frost in the air. They'd grab a coffee and then walk and talk, perhaps find a park bench to sit on.

She twisted the strap of her handbag between her fingers, as was her nervous habit. She didn't want to do this, but she also knew she had to ask him directly. It was the only way she could put her mind at rest. If she knew the truth, she could at least start to put it behind her.

She spotted Andy heading down the path towards her. It struck her again how he somehow looked no different to the boy he'd once been, even though thirty years had passed between now and then. She wondered if that was how long-time married couples remained attracted to one another, even after forty or fifty years together—they still saw each other as the young man or woman they'd first met.

"Olwen, hi." He raised his hand. "Shall I buy that coffee? It's freezing out here." He rubbed his hands together, as though to demonstrate his point.

"Yes, thanks. Just a flat white for me, please."

Andy joined the short queue and returned with their drinks a few minutes later.

"Let's walk," Olwen said, feeling as though she'd be able to think better on the move.

He nodded, and they strolled, side by side, around the park.

"I wasn't sure I'd hear from you again." He took a sip of his coffee. "You left in a rush."

"I'm sorry about last time. I guess I freaked out."

"It's okay. I understand why."

She glanced sharply at him. "Do you? Because I don't. Honestly, I'm struggling to even trust my own memory right now. I know things weren't perfect in the foster home, but I feel like I'm missing something. Like there was this big dark secret that everyone had kept from me. That's why I wanted to see you again. I want to know exactly what happened."

He pressed his lips together and stared down at his drink. "I'm not sure I can even tell you. It didn't happen to me."

"*What* didn't happen to you?" Her frustration mounted. "Why is everyone being so vague? Are you talking about the rumours of abuse? The reason the place got shut down?"

His tongue flicked out and swiped across his lower lip. "I never saw it, or experienced it for myself, but some of the others did. There was a room at the top of the house. We were told it was for storage and that it was always locked, but the truth is that storage wasn't the only thing the room was used for."

She stared at him in horror. "You're saying it's true then that someone was abusing the kids in the home? Who?"

"Like I said, I never actually experienced it for myself, and you can understand that the others didn't exactly want to talk about it."

She shook her head in disbelief. "But didn't anyone report it? Why didn't they tell someone?"

"Oh, they did. Or at least they tried to. But do you think anyone really listens to a bunch of foster kids who already have a black mark against their names? No one wanted to know. The adults always made up excuses, saying that they were imagining things or overexaggerating or simply just lying because they'd been caught fighting or drinking or something else they shouldn't have been doing."

Olwen felt sick. Child abuse had been happening all around her, and she'd had no idea. How had she missed it? Yes, she'd only been a child herself back then, but she'd considered herself close to the others. But they'd been harbouring this terrible secret all that time.

"Someone should have been arrested," she said. "They shouldn't have been allowed to just get away with it. What if this person went on and did the same thing to someone else? Why didn't the authorities deal with it?"

Andy shrugged. "If they'd prosecuted someone, it would have been all over the newspapers. The council would have been held responsible. So it was just easier to shut the place down, scatter the foster kids to the winds, and hope it all went away without a fuss."

"Jesus." She couldn't believe it, but she knew she had to.

Had her parents known? Was that why her father had reacted like he had when she'd brought the place up?

Olwen felt like her whole idea of her childhood had suddenly been rewritten. That had been the reason they'd moved house, to escape rumours of child abuse. Meanwhile, her parents had been acting completely normally around her—although they'd always been distant.

She pressed her knuckles to her lips. "I don't know what to make of all this."

"There's nothing to make of it. It's in the past now. What's done is done."

"But what about the abuser? Who was he? Was he ever prosecuted? What if he's been out there all these years, hurting other children?"

"I don't know who it was," he said, but he glanced away, towards the trees.

She wasn't sure she believed him. "How could you not have asked?"

"I told you, the ones who suffered didn't like to talk about it. They knew it would just get them in trouble, and look what happened when someone did eventually speak up? The house got shut down and we were all separated."

"Who spoke up?" she asked, though she had a feeling she already knew.

"Philip."

She took a shuddery breath. Poor Philip. He must have felt so alone.

"So Philip tried to report what had been happening, and no one believed him? No wonder he ended up feeling as though he couldn't carry on."

"He pushed us all away." Andy twisted his lips together. "I think he just wanted to put the whole thing behind him and try to live his life, but I suppose it all got too much."

She wished she knew who the abuser had been, but if Andy and the others had put it all behind them, she guessed she had no choice but to do the same.

Chapter Twenty-Nine

They'd returned to the office after gathering what information they could at the crime scene. The incident board was crowded now—photographs and maps and reports from each of the scenes lined up beside each other.

Mallory glanced up as her boss slid a fresh coffee onto her desk.

"Thought you might need this," he said.

"Thanks. I always need coffee."

He lingered by her desk.

She stared into his face and immediately knew something was troubling him. "What's wrong? What's happened?"

"I got a call to say Daniel has walked."

Mallory pressed her lips together. "I was expecting as much. I don't suppose I can do anything about it."

Ryan cleared his throat and looked away. "There's something else."

Mallory tensed. "What?"

"He's claiming you assaulted him."

Disbelief and fury filled her.

"He's what? After what he did to me? He accosted me on the street when he has a restraining order to stay away from me."

"He said bumping into you was an accident, that he didn't know you were going to be there at that time. His defence is how can he know where you're going to be in the city at all times. It's not like he went to your house."

"He's been following me! I know he has. I thought it was my imagination, that I was spooked by what happened, but I was wrong. He knew exactly where I was, and he orchestrated 'bumping' into me. I go to that corner shop all the time. The owner of the place practically knows me by name."

Ryan reached for her hand. "Hey, I believe you, Mallory. I promise I do. I'm just being straight with you. You were the one who kneed him in the balls after all, and while I can never say this for the record, I want to high five you for doing that."

"I didn't have a choice. He wanted me to run. He was like a fucking cat with a mouse, playing with me. He wanted to hurt me."

"We can't arrest people on the basis of something they haven't done."

"No, I know. I need to be dead first." She couldn't help the bitterness weaving its way into her heart. She never thought she'd be in this position. She was the detective, not the victim.

Ryan seemed to be thinking. "When's Oliver moving into the shared house?"

"He's doing a trial run there this week. Just to see how he gets on. It means if he doesn't like it, he can come home again."

Not having her brother at home was going to be weird, but she was also relieved. If Daniel was back on her case, she didn't want Oliver getting stuck in the middle of everything.

"So, move into my flat for a while," Ryan offered. "Daniel won't know you're there. It'll buy you a few days' peace at least."

She bit at her lower lip and shook her head. "I shouldn't have to move out of my own home because of that arsehole."

"I know that. I just want to help."

"You know how this works, Ryan. I never thought I would be in this position myself, but there are multiple accounts of women making repeated reports of men threatening them and even putting them in hospital, and the cases get dropped—not enough evidence to prosecute. Then the women turn up dead, and everyone asks why nothing was done, but then nothing changes." She covered her face with her hands. "The system is broken. It's fucking broken, and we're the ones who work for it."

He pulled her into a hug, and she let him.

"Let me move in with you for a while then," he offered, as they broke apart again. "If he comes anywhere near you, I'll be there."

"You can't do that. What are you going to do? Live with me for the rest of your life? It's been three months since he last attacked me. He's playing the long game. I bet he'll happily wait another three months to make sure no one is watching him, and then he'll make his move." She let out a sigh. "I know it's in your nature to want to protect everyone, Ryan, but sometimes you just have to accept that you can't."

Chapter Thirty

There was nothing Ryan hated more than feeling helpless.
It was one of the things that had driven his OCD—that need to control his surroundings. He'd felt helpless in the wake of his daughter's death, unable to offer any kind of comfort to his grieving wife, to lessen her pain in any way, and he'd experienced the same emotions when the young man who'd killed Hayley had been handed a pathetic excuse for a sentence.

Now, he could sense his brain fire up again, urging his repetitive behaviours. The urge to count, or tap, or check something repeatedly buzzed in his head. He didn't want to go back there again, but what would stop it?

He'd dealt with Hayley's killer, hadn't he? Maybe he needed to do the same with Daniel Williamson?

No, he couldn't. Getting himself fired and locked up wasn't going to help anyone. Plus, he had a responsibility to the families of the victims of his current case to find whoever had murdered them. He was also concerned that if they didn't find the perpetrator soon, there might even be a fourth family who would lose a loved one in such a horrific way.

Considering Daniel Williamson's history, Mallory wasn't going to face suspension while the incident was investigated, but he still worried that Daniel would do or say whatever he could to drag her down with him. Why the fuck couldn't men like him just leave women alone and go on and live their lives? Their skin was so thin and fragile that the slightest rebuke cut right down to their cowardly hearts, and they made it their mission to make that woman pay.

The new recruit, DC Grewal, drew Ryan's attention. Grewal approached Ryan's desk, almost bouncing on the tips of his toes in his excitement.

On his return to the office, Ryan had focused the majority of his team on learning more about the history of each of the victims. DCI Hirst had most of the office working on this case now, so Ryan was able to put other detectives onto jobs like scrolling through CCTV and speaking to witnesses. Pretty soon, the national press would link the three deaths together, and then they'd be swarmed with reporters as well as everything else.

"Boss," Grewal said, "I think I've found a link. It might be a tenuous one, but it's something."

Ryan sat back. "I'll take anything at this point."

"Thirty years ago, Gary Carter used to work as a carer in a kids' foster home in Redland. I've gone back as far as I can, but it looks like victim number three might have been involved with the social care side of things, placing kids into foster homes and that kind of thing."

Ryan tapped his pen against his desk. "You think they might have known each other all those years ago?"

"It has to be a possibility, right?"

"But what about the second victim, Jillian Griffiths?"

"The link for this one was harder to pin down. I dug deep into their backgrounds, including into the foster home where Carter used to work when he was in his twenties. It turns out, the place was shut down after only a couple of years amid accusations of drug dealing and anti-social behaviour, though no one was prosecuted. The neighbours didn't like the place."

Redland was an affluent area now, though it might have been different thirty years ago. Either way, he could understand why the locals might not have been happy about having a foster home on their doorsteps.

"Okay," Ryan said slowly, still not seeing the link with the second victim. "And what did you find?"

"I was going through old newspaper articles about the place. One of the neighbours gave an interview and slated the place, saying how the kids were out of control, involved in drink and drugs, stealing and fighting, basically bringing the neighbourhood into disrepute. Guess what her name was?"

"Jillian Griffiths," Ryan guessed.

"Exactly."

"Excellent work, Grewal. That must be it. I don't know why someone is choosing to kill them now, but it's a start. That foster home must be the connection."

Ryan got to his feet and commanded the attention of the rest of his team. He filled them in on what Grewal had discovered, making sure he mentioned the young detective as being the one responsible for finding the link. This achievement would do the world of good for Grewal's self-confidence and help to bond him to the rest of the team, make him feel like he'd earned his place.

"We have to take into account that these people have had their tongues removed and their mouths sewn shut," Ryan told his team. "Is someone trying to keep them quiet? Perhaps something happened at the foster home all those years ago?"

"Why now?" Mallory asked. "What could they possibly have to say that hadn't already been said back then?"

Ryan shook his head. "Honestly, I'm not sure. But our killer must be connected to that foster home. I want the names of every single person connected to it, from the kids who lived there, to the people who worked there, or even those who might have visited or been involved in placing the children, like Victoria Fletcher. Any names we can pull up might be one of two things. They could either be potential victims, or we might even be looking at our killer."

Everyone who'd been murdered had been older, so it wasn't as though one of the previous foster children had been targeted. Was that because it was one of them who was responsible for the deaths?

Across the office, fingers flew over keyboards, and phone calls were made. It didn't take long before his sergeant got his attention.

"The home was opened up by a married couple," Mallory said, "Elanor and Charles Morgan. Elanor passed away a couple of years ago, and Charles Morgan is now in a home himself, suffering from Alzheimer's, so I'm not sure what use he'll be to us as far as questioning goes."

"At least we can rule him out as a suspect." Ryan tapped his fingers against his thigh, fighting the urge to count.

"Elanor and Charles did have a daughter. Her name is Olwen Morgan, and she's local."

"She might be in danger. We definitely need to talk to her. Have we got a recent address?"

Mallory checked her notes. "Yes, she lives in a flat in Kingswood. She's also listed as an accountant at a firm in the city."

Ryan glanced at his watch. It was two p.m. on a weekday. If Olwen Morgan was a professional woman, there was a good chance they'd be more likely to catch her at work than at home.

"Let's try the office first," he suggested. "If she's not there, we'll go to her home after."

WITHIN TWENTY MINUTES, they drove into the small car park outside an office block. The building had been divided up between several different businesses, and each of the car park spaces had small signs indicating which ones had been allocated to which company.

Ryan pulled into one of the spots for the accountancy firm and switched off the engine. He and Mallory climbed out, and they approached the main doors and entered into the warmth of the interior.

A young receptionist at the front desk smiled at them. "Good afternoon. Can I help you?"

"We need to speak with Olwen Morgan at Watson Accountancy."

"Do you have an appointment?"

Ryan took his ID from the inside of his jacket pocket and held it up for her to see. "It's a police matter."

The young woman's expression changed, and she blinked. This time, her smile was more reserved. "I see. Give me one sec, and I'll see if she's available."

They let the receptionist do her job, calling up to the accountancy firm.

"It's on floor three," she told them. "Miss Morgan is expecting you."

Ryan thanked her, and they caught the lift up to the correct floor.

A woman in her forties, in a dark-grey business suit, was waiting to greet them. Her blonde hair was poker straight and held back from her face with a clip. She stared at them from behind a pair of glasses.

"I'm Olwen Morgan" she said, before they'd even had the chance to introduce themselves. "What's this about?"

Her tone was curt and cold, and Ryan picked up a defensiveness behind it. This woman knew something, though he wasn't sure what yet.

"Do you have an office we can speak in?" he asked.

She nodded. "Follow me."

Her office was tidy and a little sparse. There wasn't even a pot plant. No photographs of children or any other kind of family on the desk. It might be her office, but anyone could have been using it.

She gestured for them to take a seat on the other side of the desk. "What's this about?"

Matching her direct approach, Ryan jumped straight in. "We need to talk to you about the foster home that your parents ran in the nineties."

Was it his imagination, or did the mention of it have her shifting in her chair?

She straightened her spine and laced her fingers together on the desk in front of her. "What about it? It was a very long time ago."

"We're currently investigating three murders. You may have read about them in the news? One where a man was left drugged on a train track, another was a woman pushed off a bridge onto a motorway, and the third was killed early this morning after being pushed in front of a bus."

Miss Morgan paled. "That's terrible, but what does it have to do with the foster home?"

He responded to her question with one of his own. "Do you know these names? Gary Carter, Jillian Griffiths, and Victoria Fletcher?"

The woman blinked. "I-I'm not sure."

"They were each connected with the foster home in some way. Gary worked there when he was in his twenties, before it was shut down, Jillian was one of your neighbours, and Victoria was a social worker. We believe she may have been responsible for placing some of the children who lived there."

"I can hardly be expected to remember the names of people loosely connected with the place. I was a child myself back then."

"How old were you when the foster home was open?" Ryan asked.

"I was fourteen when it was first set up. I think I was sixteen when we moved and the place shut down again."

"Your father is still alive, is that right?" Ryan checked. "I'd like to speak with him, if at all possible."

Her entire body seemed to stiffen at the mention of her father. "He's alive, but he won't be any good to you. He's suffering with Alzheimer's, and he's in a home. He won't remember anything."

Ryan got the impression she was trying to protect her father. Perhaps that was only natural, when the old man was vulnerable, but maybe there was more to it.

"Did he ever talk about the foster home?" Ryan asked.

Ms Morgan shook her head. "No, never. Once we'd moved, it was like the place had never existed."

"Can you think of any reason why someone might have wanted to keep the people connected to the home quiet?"

Her tongue swiped across her lips, and she glanced away again. There was definitely something she was holding back.

"Miss Morgan?" Ryan prompted.

She drew a shaky breath. "I don't know how much truth there is in it, but I've learned there were abuse allegations surrounding the foster home."

"Abuse allegations?" Ryan repeated. "By whom?"

She shook her head. "Honestly, I'm not completely sure. I didn't know anything about it until just this week. Have you tried talking to any of the other residents who were there at the time? They probably know a hell of a lot more than I do."

Ryan narrowed his eyes. Was she deliberately trying to redirect him away from her and her father?

"Are you in touch with any of them?"

"Only recently," she admitted. "I bumped into Andy—Andrew—Hallam a week or so ago. I hadn't seen him for years. We went for a drink, and he brought a couple of the others along."

Ryan angled his head. "Which others?"

"Samuel Newton and Tina Cole."

Beside him, Mallory scribbled down the names in her notebook.

"They were still in touch then?"

She nodded. "With each other, yes."

"What was the impression you got of Andrew Hallam?"

"He was friendly. Welcoming. He seemed pleased to see me." Her features twisted in concern. "You don't think he's the one responsible, do you? He's not a suspect in these murders?"

"Why would you assume that?"

She glanced down at her hands. "I'm not sure."

"We're simply exploring all options right now," Ryan tried to reassure her. "Can you give me the names of the other foster children who were there at the time?"

"Umm...some of them...I think. There were the ones I already told you about, but also Wesley Kinnon and Anita Miyares. A boy called Philip Ross lived there, too, but he committed suicide after the home was shut down."

"I'm sorry to hear that," Mallory said with a sympathetic smile.

Olwen glanced down at her desk. "I was, too. He was a good kid."

"There's something else I need to ask you about," Ryan said. "The victims all had their tongues cut out and their lips sewn shut."

The colour drained from Miss Morgan's face. "What?"

"To us, it indicates that someone is trying to keep them quiet. Or perhaps someone is trying to send out a message to someone else to keep their mouths shut. Does this mean anything to you?"

She looked between the two detectives, shock written all over her face. "You think someone is trying to keep a secret to do with the alleged abuse happening in the foster home? A secret from thirty years ago?"

"Could that be a possibility?"

She pressed her lips together and nodded. "Yes, it could."

Ryan leaned forwards slightly. "Is it possible the person responsible for the abuse is now killing those who knew their name? Do *you* know this person's name?"

She shook her head. "No. Like I said, I didn't even know there had been rumours of abuse until very recently."

"Until you met with Andrew Hallam?" Ryan checked.

"Exactly."

"Did you ever wonder if the person doing the abusing might have been one of the other foster children rather than someone who worked there?"

She blinked behind her glasses. "No, that never occurred to me. I mean, they were children."

"They were teenagers. Some of them approaching sixteen years old. It's not as though physically they were children."

Her expression crumpled. "I-I never thought of it that way."

"Were there any other adults connected with the place whose names you can think of?"

Her forehead creased. "Why? Might they be in danger, too?"

"Potentially."

Ms Morgan thought for a moment. "Other people worked there, but I don't know their names, I'm sorry. It was so long ago." She straightened, her shoulders tensing. "There's my aunt, but she stayed away from the place. She didn't like it from the start."

"What's your aunt's name?" Ryan asked.

She gave it to them, and Mallory took it down, together with her address and contact details.

"You don't think Aunt Milly might be in any danger, do you?" She was clearly distressed now. "She really didn't have anything to do with the place."

Ryan linked his fingers together. "I'm afraid we can't be sure about anything right now. Do you live alone, Ms Morgan?"

"Yes, why?"

"Is there anyone you can stay with for a week or so?"

She shook her head. "Not really. Why? Do you think I'm in some kind of danger?"

"I think it would be a sensible precaution."

"No one has got any reason to want me dead," she said. "I've never done anything to anyone."

He exhaled a breath. "As far as we can tell, neither did the victims, but that didn't stop someone from killing them."

Ryan reached into his pocket and then placed a business card on the desk in front of her. "That's everything for now. If you think of anything else that might help us with our investigations, or if you're concerned about anything, don't hesitate to call. I do want you to take this seriously, Miss Morgan. Three people are dead."

"I understand."

The detectives excused themselves and left the office.

"What do you make of her?" Ryan asked Mallory in the lift on the way down.

"I don't think she's our killer, if that's what you're asking. For one, there's no way she'd be physically strong enough to get drugged adults to the locations."

The lift pinged, and the doors opened out onto the lobby. The two detectives stepped out.

Ryan was still mulling everything over. "Do you think it's a coincidence that she bumped into one of the old residents on the same week that people connected to the foster home started to be murdered?"

Mallory glanced over at him. "You think Andrew Hallam orchestrated to bump into her?"

"I'm not sure, but I think it's a possibility we need to consider. We definitely need to talk to him, and anyone else who lived there that we can track down."

"The kids came and went. We could be looking at a fair number of people, and they could be anywhere now."

"We still need to find them, even if it's only to rule them out. Find out where they were at the time of each murder, and if they have an alibi. Let's start with the ones Olwen Morgan was able to name, and then narrow them down."

"I'll try and pull their records," Mallory said.

They reached the building door, and Ryan reached out to open it. "I think Andrew Hallam needs to be our first port of call."

"Agreed."

As they got back to the pool car, Ryan drew to a halt.

"Look," he said, jerking his chin across the car park. "Where do you think she's going?"

Mallory followed his line of sight. "I'm not sure, but she certainly seems in a hurry."

They watched as Olwen Morgan climbed into a mustard-yellow Kia Picanto and drove away as though someone was chasing her.

Chapter Thirty-One

Olwen's world had somehow become both stiflingly small and overwhelmingly huge all at the same time. She wanted to lock herself away and hide, while also feeling compelled to run as far and fast as she could.

She'd made her excuses to her boss, claiming a family emergency, and left the office. She drove too fast, swearing each time she hit a red light, throwing her hands up at drivers who were barely even going the speed limit. Was her life really in danger? The details the detective had shared of how the previous victims had died sickened her. Those poor people. She didn't know what they'd done or what reason someone had for wanting them dead, but she knew no one deserved to die like that.

She wanted to go home and lock the front door, but perhaps she should listen to the detectives and find somewhere else to stay for the time being. Would a killer really come to her house? Did she know them? What if it was someone she trusted and she let them walk right through the front door? The thought made her hot and sweaty, her heart palpitating, while also chilling her to her core. Perhaps Aunt Millie would let her come and stay for a week or so, at least until the police caught whoever was doing this.

What if Aunt Millie knew something? She might be in danger, too.

Olwen's head was spinning. This was all too much.

Had Andrew Hallam deliberately bumped into her?

Surely, if the police thought Andy was a danger, then they'd have arrested him already? And what about the others? If it could be Andy, then why not one of them? Well, maybe not one of the women, but could one of the men have killed those people? She remembered how Wesley Kinnon had always been the troublemaker back then, the one who'd punched holes in the walls and got into fights with the others. Then there was Samuel. He'd been the type of kid who you almost expected to hear of torturing insects or the neighbourhood cat. Maybe he was the one responsible?

Or maybe the killer wasn't even anyone who used to live there. Couldn't it just be a coincidence that each of the victims had a connection to the home? Jillian Griffiths had only been a neighbour. That was a weak connection at best.

Olwen tried to remember the woman. She could recall maybe a couple of interactions, but she couldn't place any kind of face to the name. It had been such a long time ago, and her memory was spotty. She found it hard to imagine the woman had done anything that might result in her being brutally murdered thirty years later.

Her fingers itched to get on the phone to talk to someone about this, but she didn't know who. Who could she even trust? She was sure she could trust her aunt, but bringing up the subject of the foster home once more left her uneasy. Her aunt had never held back in voicing her opinions about the place. Wouldn't this just prove her right? That it could still come back to haunt them thirty years later?

Olwen knew she needed to talk to Aunt Millicent. If something happened to her aunt, and Olwen could have said or done something to prevent it, she'd never forgive herself.

Didn't she say she had a man now? A younger one, at that. Aunt Milly wasn't alone, and Olwen didn't want to ask to stay and become a spare part. Three was company and all that.

She needed to check on her father, too. If someone was killing people connected to the foster home, then surely that put her dad at the top of the hit list? It wasn't as though her father could even defend himself in his condition, but the sick fuck who was doing this probably didn't care. Olwen tried to reassure herself that the care home was covered in security cameras and there were plenty of staff who would watch out for him.

Even so, worry clutched at her heart, and she knew she wouldn't be able to breathe again until she'd checked on him. She wanted to warn the staff at the care home as well. It wasn't that she wanted to frighten them, but they needed to be aware of the connection between her father and the recent spate of murders in the city.

The drive felt as though it took forever, but finally she pulled into the care home car park and jumped out of the car. She was in such a rush, she didn't even bother to pick up her handbag, and instead hurried to the entrance and hit the button beside the door to be buzzed in.

Her heart beat too fast, and her mouth had run dry. The adrenaline that had been coursing through her body ever since her conversation with the detectives hadn't abated. She glanced over her shoulder, half expecting to find Andrew Hallam standing behind her with a knife in one hand and a sewing needle in the other.

She shook her head at herself. This wasn't a horror film.

The doors buzzed open, and Olwen went straight to reception. One of the young female carers sat behind the desk, and she threw Olwen a warm, welcoming smile as she approached.

"Ms Morgan, hi. Your father is popular today. He already has a visitor."

"He does?" Alarm bells instantly rang inside her. No one came to visit her father except her. "Who?"

"He said he's one of the kids your father used to foster. He's only in the area for today and thought he'd drop in. Isn't that lovely? I had no idea your parents used to foster. I'll be honest, he never really seemed like the type."

Olwen knew what 'type' she meant. The loving, nurturing kind of person who invites an unwanted, unloved child into their home—a child who, most likely, was going to have issues of their own—and show them what it was like to have a normal family life. She wished she'd experienced this woman's idea of what a foster carer should be like, rather than the strange, businesslike situation she'd grown up in. The irony was that she hadn't even been one of the foster kids, but yet she felt like she had. Her home growing up hadn't been full of warmth and love and laughter. In fact, she'd spent most of her life depressingly lonely, and she hadn't even realised it. It was the same loneliness that had followed her through into adulthood.

"Did you catch his name?" Olwen asked.

The carer took the visitor's book and pushed it towards Olwen. "Here, I got him to sign in."

Olwen tugged the book towards her and ran her finger down the page until she got to the correct entry. The words were no more than a scribble and completely illegible. Had they done that on purpose to hide their identity?

"Is something wrong?" the young woman asked.

"I can't read that name. I need to make sure my father is okay."

The carer looked concerned now, her eyebrows pinching together, her lips folding into a thin line. "Why wouldn't he be?"

How could she possibly explain? Someone was murdering people who were connected to the foster home thirty years ago. He was a helpless old man. Why would someone want to hurt him? But then why had someone hurt those other people, too? What had the neighbour ever done to deserve what had happened to her, or the man who'd worked at the home? Or the old social worker? Wasn't her father as likely to be a victim as any of them?

Could it be that Andrew Hallam was the abuser and he'd been killing off anyone who knew that about him?

Olwen couldn't explain right now. She needed to make sure her father was safe.

She left the reception area at a run, garnering curious glances from everyone she passed. She reached his room, and, without bothering to knock, slammed through the door. Her heart felt like it was in her throat and head, the beat pounding on the insides of her ears.

"Dad?"

She drew up short. Her father was in his usual chair. A man sat opposite him. Her first thought was that thank God her father was okay, her second was that it wasn't Andrew in the other chair.

It was Samuel Cole.

She blinked. "Sam? What are you doing here?"

Sam frowned at her. "You okay, Olwen? You seem kind of flustered."

"I am flustered!" Her fear had turned to anger. "What the fuck are you doing here?"

"Jeez, there's no need to be like that. I wanted to come and say hello to your father. After I saw you the other day, I thought it would be nice to see the old man again."

She frowned. "How did you find out where he was?"

"You told us when we were having drinks the other night."

"Did I?"

She couldn't remember telling them the name of the care home, but she may well have. She had talked about him, telling the others that he wasn't doing so well, and that he was in a residential home now. She hadn't known there was any reason to hide that information at that point.

Though her father was unharmed, she still didn't completely trust Sam. Maybe he just hadn't got around to hurting her father yet. If she'd arrived another ten minutes later, would she have been walking in on a completely different scene?

Despite everything, she still had to fight against her instinct to be polite. Her doubt in herself was enough that she worried she was being rude to someone who didn't deserve it.

"I'm sorry, Sam, but I'm really going to have to ask you to leave. Now's not a good time."

Sam frowned, his lips thinning. "Oh, right. Of course." He raised his voice and patted her dad on the knee. "It was good to see you again, Mr Morgan."

The old man's milky blue eyes darted from side to side, as though he deliberately didn't want to look at Sam. Had Sam done or said something before she'd arrived that had made him uncomfortable? Or did her father have another reason to not enjoy the company of his past ward?

Sam got to his feet and nodded at Olwen. "Apologies if I've upset you for some reason."

"Just go."

Had the police not contacted Sam? Did he not know what was going on? The truth danced on the tip of her tongue, but she couldn't bring herself to say anything. She had no reason to trust this man.

Olwen stepped out of the way, allowing him to leave. She gave it a couple of seconds and then glanced back at her father.

"I'll be back in a bit, Dad, okay? I won't be long."

She wanted to make sure Sam had left the building. She didn't want him hiding out in one of the toilets or something, waiting for her to go so he could make his move.

She followed him down the corridor, staying just far back enough that he wouldn't notice her. She waited until he'd left via the main doors and then allowed herself to take a breath. Her hands trembled. It was as though she could suddenly see danger everywhere.

Should she phone the police and tell them that she'd found Samuel Cole in her father's room? They should know. If they had something on him, it might help them decide whether they should bring him in for questioning.

She stopped at the reception desk to let the staff know her father wasn't to have any other visitors other than her, and then made her way back out to her car. She'd been in such a rush, she'd left her handbag in the footwell of the passenger seat, and it contained both her phone and the card the handsome detective had given her. She fumbled for her car keys in her pocket and then realised she hadn't even remembered to lock the doors in her haste to get to her father's room.

Olwen opened the driver's door, slid behind the wheel, and then reached down into the footwell for her bag.

Before she even had the chance to pick it up, something clear and plastic fell over the top of her head, and suddenly, she couldn't breathe.

Chapter Thirty-Two

Olwen woke with a gasp. She clawed at her face, still half expecting to find the plastic bag that had restricted her airways to be there, but her fingers only found skin.

The light in the room was dim, and she glanced around and instantly recoiled. Numerous sets of glassy eyes stared down at her from the walls, and there were yet more on every surface. Furry, feathered, or scaled—the type of animal didn't seem to matter. They all adorned the space.

The head of some kind of antelope stared down at her, its horns coiled and sharp. A maned wolf, styled as though it was snarling, revealed its white pointed teeth. A warthog, with tusks jutting from the sides of its hideous snout, was forever frozen in position. There were so many more creatures mounted on the walls, but that wasn't the end of it. On the tables and side units, smaller animals jostled for prime position—squirrels and hares, a bat and a fox, and birds of every shape and size.

Where the hell was she?

She needed to get out of here. Even if she hadn't just been half suffocated and abducted, she would have been afraid waking up in this room. Who did it belong to? She looked for a door or a window, any way out.

Had Samuel Cole waited for her by her car and attacked her when she'd tried to get her phone from her bag? Had he also murdered those other people? It made sense.

That bastard.

She wasn't tied up, which she took as a good thing. She didn't quite feel herself, though. She told herself it was because of the lack of oxygen, yet when she tried to get her legs to cooperate to get her to the door, they didn't respond.

A fresh shot of adrenaline went through her. Was she paralysed? Had the lack of oxygen to her brain permanently disabled her?

But she glanced down, and, upon willing her legs to move, they did. She opened and closed her fists, and a small trickle of relief and hope went through her. Not paralysed then, her limbs just didn't seem to want to do what she told them.

Had he drugged her?

She did feel woozy. She'd put it down to her just regaining consciousness, but it might be more. Something was definitely wrong with her arms and legs.

She hunted around for her bag, desperately hoping to find it somewhere close by, but of course, it was nowhere to be found. He wasn't stupid enough to leave her in here with her phone.

Where was Sam? Was he somewhere close by? She wished she knew where this house was, had some picture of what surrounded her. If she could get her limbs to move, and get out of the door, she might be able to go to a neighbour for help, or at least flag down a car.

Olwen opened her mouth and tried her tongue, though it felt too big and fat. "Hellll…"

The word was long and slurred, but it was a word, and she'd almost formed it.

She tried again. "Heeelllppp."

It was louder this time, her voice growing stronger. Maybe whatever he'd given her was wearing off.

Emboldened by the thought, Olwen put some more effort into getting her arms and legs to respond. It was as though she'd been lying on them and they'd gone to sleep. She needed to get everything working before he came back.

What would happen to her if she was still like this when he did? She remembered the detective's description of the previous victims, how he'd cut out their tongues and sewn up their mouths before murdering them. Was that going to be her fate?

Hundreds of little glass eyes seemed to watch her every move. She shuddered, sensing herself shrinking under their scrutiny.

Was Samuel into this shit? Or had he brought her to someone else's house?

She needed to get out of here.

Olwen opened and closed her hands, trying to get feeling back into them. Whatever she'd been given was wearing off by the minute, but it still felt like too long.

Finally, she managed to raise her arms and grab hold of the side of a table and used it to haul herself to standing. The movement knocked over one of the pieces of taxidermy—a mouse positioned on a piece of wood to make it look like a log—and it fell to the floor and broke.

Her legs didn't feel like her own, but at least she was standing now. She estimated it would take her about ten steps to get from here to the door. She had no idea what lay beyond, but at least she'd be out of this horrible room.

What if he was waiting on the other side for her? This all might be some sick game to him.

It didn't matter. She would deal with it when it happened. She couldn't let her fear hold her back. If she did, it might kill her.

Olwen got her legs to move, though it felt like both feet had been embedded in concrete blocks. She used the furniture to pull herself along, not caring how many of the awful statues she knocked over or damaged. She felt bad for all the living animals they'd once been, to have been turned into something so grotesque.

She was almost there. Just a few more steps. She could do this.

Movement came in the doorway, and, a moment later, a man stepped into the room.

Olwen let out a squeak of terror and lost her balance.

She hit one of the sideboards on her way down, scattering the stuffed animals all around her.

She stared up at the man's face, hardly able to believe what she was seeing.

It wasn't Samuel.

Though it had been thirty years since she'd last seen him, she'd have recognised him anywhere. His almost-black hair was closer to grey now, and there were lines around his brown eyes, but he still somehow looked the same.

"Philip? I-I don't understand. I thought you were dead."

The man took a step farther into the room. "Philip *is* dead, or at least I tried to make it that way. I thought I'd buried him, but then Gary Carter got in touch and brought Philip back to life."

Her mind blurred. What was he talking about? How was it possible to bring someone back to life? It wasn't.

"Wh—what do you want with me?"

"To make sure you understand what you did."

What was she supposed to have done?

"No, please, don't hurt me," she begged.

He took another step, and she pushed herself back across the floor with her feet. Fallen taxidermy statues scattered around her. She picked one up and tried to throw it at him, but her motor skills still weren't that good, and it just toppled back to the floor.

"Help!" she screamed. "Someone, help me."

Thank God her voice was working again.

He produced a scalpel from behind his back. "I wouldn't do that if I were you. You're only going to make me want to silence you quicker."

She clamped her lips together.

"You don't want to lose your tongue? Do you?"

Desperately, she shook her head.

He motioned with the scalpel. "You can speak. Just don't scream again, or I will slice your tongue out of your head."

"What do you want from me?" she sobbed.

"I want to teach you a lesson."

"Like you did the others, you mean? Why did you do that to them? Were you trying to keep them quiet?" Did this mean Philip was the abuser and he'd been trying to shut anyone up who knew about him? It didn't make sense. "Why would any of them say anything after all these years?"

He stared at her, his lip curled in derision, his nostrils flared. "Is that what you think? That I was trying to keep them quiet?"

"Why else cut out their tongues and sew up their mouths like that?"

"It was punishment, but not because they'd opened their mouths when they shouldn't."

"What then?"

"It was their punishment for keeping them shut and not telling people the truth about what was happening in that house."

She blinked back tears. "That house? The foster home, you mean? What happened?"

"Your mother was an abuser. A monster. And everyone covered for her."

Olwen's head was spinning. Her mother? "What are you talking about?"

"She was abusing boys at the foster home, boys including me. I suspect I was her favourite. Your father knew all about it, too."

"No, that's not true."

"Yes, it is, Olwen. Why do you think they set that place up? They didn't need the money. They both had good careers. You know they were hardly the caring types who actually wanted to take care of a bunch of teenagers. They didn't even want to look after their own daughter."

Olwen blinked back tears. "I don't believe you."

He huffed air out through his nose. "Why doesn't that surprise me. No one believed me."

She shook her head. "No."

"Don't you remember that room upstairs where we weren't allowed to go? That was where she took me when it was time for some *fun*. Maybe if it had been girls she'd been abusing, things would have been different. I'd have been listened to. But a smoking, drinking, fighting teenage boy claiming that a forty-year-old woman was having sex with him sounded like wishful thinking."

"I don't believe you," she said again.

She wanted to scream. Her entire mental and emotional image of her mother had been completely torn to shreds in a matter of minutes. Did she believe Philip?

Now she looked back, there were too many moments where her parents had been acting strangely. No wonder they hadn't wanted her to have anything to do with the kids next door. She always thought it was because they hadn't wanted their teenage daughter to get involved with one of the boys and be led astray, but it was because they hadn't wanted her to get close enough to one of them that they'd confide in her.

Did Aunt Milly know? No, Olwen was sure she hadn't known what was happening, but she'd sensed something was off. Milly had always blamed Olwen's father, but actually, her sister was to blame.

Philip wasn't done. "That fucking room has haunted my dreams my whole life. Even when I tried to become someone else, I couldn't leave it behind me."

"No."

"How can you still deny this, Olwen? You saw us in there. You walked in on us."

She shook her head. "You're lying. I'd remember something like that."

"That's just typical of you, isn't it? Something didn't fit your view of life, so you just cut it out of your mind. Erased it from your memory."

"I-I—"

She didn't want to believe him, and yet his words stirred something inside her. Hadn't she said herself that she felt as though she was missing chunks of time from back then?

"Your mother told me I should be grateful. She said lots of teenage boys would give anything to be in my shoes. A teenage boy with an attractive older woman. But it sickened me. I knew it wasn't right. And that you and your father just stood by and watched it all happening made things even worse."

Olwen blinked back tears. "But I didn't. I had no idea."

He slammed down his hand, and she jumped.

"Liar! You walked in on us that day. You knew exactly what was happening. You turned around and ran out again."

"No..." she whispered.

He continued, "I was so confused. I told myself that I must have wanted it, because if I didn't, I wouldn't have got hard when she touched me. She took my hand and made me touch her, too. I would be able to smell her on my fingers, and I'd run to the toilet and throw up. Your father got off on it, too. He enjoyed watching her rape me, because that's what she did. I was fifteen years old. She treated me like some kind of sex toy, to be used whenever she wanted it. The other boys would tease me, saying she was hot, and even joking about what it would be like to have sex with her. They didn't know it was actually happening to me."

Olwen thought she was going to vomit. "Oh God."

Tears shimmered in his dark eyes. "I tried to tell people. The first person was that nice neighbour, only she turned out to be not so nice. I thought she would tell someone and get me some help, but she stayed silent, just like they all did in the end. Instead of helping me, she avoided me."

"I'm so sorry," Olwen whispered.

"Do you remember Gary Carter? He walked in on us once, too. She was sitting on top of me, naked from the waist down. He saw us, and his eyes went wide, and he flushed bright red. But he didn't try to stop her. He just apologised and backed out of the room. Do you think it would have been that way if he'd walked in on your father raping one of the girls? Do you think he'd have apologised and left?"

"I don't know," she said, but she knew the truth. Something would have been done.

"I tried to talk to him about it, to tell him I didn't want it, and that she made me do it, but he just kind of nudged me with his elbow, and did this whole 'ha-ha, of course you didn't' thing, like it was all some kind of fucking joke. He thought I should be happy I had a woman more than twice my age having sex with me. As for that fucking bitch of a social worker, Jillian Griffiths, I should have killed her a long time ago. I went to her and asked to move, and when she asked why, I said Mrs Morgan was acting inappropriately towards me, and do you know what she did? She made me sit down with your mother, with her in the room as well, and made me tell her that I didn't want to have sex with her anymore. Of course, I couldn't say it, so she called me a liar."

Olwen swallowed hard and fought back tears.

"That's why I made them silent for good." He carried on, "I took their tongues and sewed up their lips. If they wanted to keep my secret, they could take it to the grave."

Chapter Thirty-Three

Everyone in the office was hard at work, pulling everything they could about the foster home Elanor and Charles Morgan had run in the nineties.

Shonda approached his desk. "I think I've found something, boss."

"Let's hear it."

"I've been working my way through the teenagers who were registered as staying at the foster home in the nineties. I've got six different names. We've managed to track down three of them so far: Andrew Hallam, Tina Newton, and Samuel Cole. The three who Olwen Morgan met up with recently. We haven't been able to find Wesley Kinnon, and one of the other girls—well, woman now—emigrated to Australia twenty years ago. There is one other name that caught my attention. Philip Ross. When I was searching his background, I found an article that said he'd committed suicide by hanging, but when I dug a bit deeper, I couldn't find an actual death certificate for him."

"Okay," Ryan said, prompting her to get to the point.

"Here's the interesting bit. In actual fact, he didn't die at all. I found a record of him changing his name. It happened a few days after he apparently 'died'."

That was interesting. What reason would someone have for wanting to make people believe they were dead?

Shonda continued, "So a quick search on the name Philip Ross would show that he'd died. Unless a person knew to dig deeper, they'd take it at face value. He didn't have any family to prove otherwise."

"He wanted to vanish. But why?" Ryan tapped his fingers to his lips. "What's his name now?"

"Bryce Ogden. No previous convictions. But get this—he works as a taxidermist."

Ryan raised both eyebrows. "A taxidermist? So, he'd know how to sew?"

"Exactly. There's something else. I ran his name against the information we took from the victims' laptops and tablets, and learned that Gary Carter had contacted Philip—Bryce—three months ago after his dog died."

"That's right. I remember all the dog items we found in his home," Ryan said. "It looked like he couldn't let go, even though the dog had been dead a while."

"Well, looks like he really thought he couldn't let go of the animal because he contacted Philip about stuffing his dead dog."

Ryan rubbed his hand across his mouth. "Jesus Christ. Why would someone want to do that to their pet?"

"He didn't go ahead with it, obviously. From the emails, it was actually Philip—Bryce—who talked him out of it, saying that when it came to pets, time was a better healer. But my guess is that Philip must have recognised the name. Maybe he even arranged to meet up or something, I'm not sure yet."

"They knew each other," Ryan filled in. "They knew each other from all those years ago."

"That's right. Maybe Philip used it as an excuse to stop him and get him to talk, or have a coffee, and spiked him with the Rohypnol then."

"That's excellent work, Detective."

Shonda beamed.

A light pinged on in Ryan's head, and he swivelled back to his computer. He did a quick search to find out what kind of stuffing a taxidermist might use. He read through the information as quickly as he could. It appeared that several different materials could be used, including sawdust and foam, but there was one fibre in particular that caught his eye.

"Woodwool," he said out loud.

"Sorry, boss?" Shonda said.

"Taxidermists sometimes use it, and it was found at two of our scenes. My guess is that it's found at the third scene, too, once it's been properly processed."

"You think Bryce Ogden is our man?"

"I do. Where is he based?"

"He's local. He has a place on the outskirts of Bristol, only two miles from the part of the track where the first victim was killed."

"Shit. We need to get out there, now."

Ryan jumped to his feet and filled his team in on the latest discovery. "We need to put a team together to go out to Bryce Ogden's property asap."

He went to Mandy Hirst's office and filled his DCI in on what they'd learned.

"Good work," she told him. "It certainly sounds like you've got the right man."

"We haven't got him, yet."

She gave him a smile of encouragement. "Then what are you waiting for? Go catch that bastard."

Chapter Thirty-Four

Expressionless eyes stared down at him from every wall. Even in the dim light, the glass reflected his image.

Though he knew they couldn't see, Philip still felt as though they followed his every move. They were his companions, his pets, his family. They never let him down, or mocked him, or made him promises they knew they wouldn't keep.

They *listened*.

His most recent piece of work was a bird—a beautiful tawny owl—its feathers as soft as silk.

People often thought the animals would somehow remain warm and soft, as they were in life, but that was far from the reality. Once completed, their bodies were hard and cold, unmoving. They were set in the position for the rest of their days.

His first ever piece of work had been an experiment. He'd found a cat on the road that must have only recently been hit by a car. Other than a tiny amount of blood around its nose and mouth, it looked as though it was sleeping.

He'd picked it up, shocked at the strange, loose, lifelessness to its body. But something had gone through him then, catching his breath and making his heart race faster.

There had been no life in the poor creature, and yet he'd felt a connection to it. He'd stroked its soft fur then tucked it inside his jacket. He'd glanced around, ensuring there was no one nearby to see him. The road had been empty, so he'd quickly got back inside his car and driven home.

It hadn't taken long to find what he'd needed on the internet. He'd put the cat in his fridge to keep it cool and then ordered the equipment.

He'd botched that particular project. Perhaps he shouldn't have been surprised, but he'd cried over the loss of the animal as though it had been his own much-loved pet.

It had never even occurred to him that someone else might have been missing the cat. It wasn't until he'd seen a poster stuck to a lamppost offering a reward for a return of 'Ginger' that it had hit him. Instead of feeling sorry for the family, he'd been filled with a sense of jealousy, angry that someone else had tried to claim the animal when it was clearly his.

He hadn't been Philip anymore at that point. Philip had been dead for some time. He'd been Bryce Ogden—a name he was sure no one would ever link to him—and had put Philip and what had happened to that poor boy behind him.

After that experience, he'd spent more time online, asking questions in forums, posting pictures of his work to get the opinions of others in the craft. It soon became clear that he had a talent, a way of bringing these dead creatures back to life.

When the first person contacted him to commission a piece of work—a prize carp someone had caught—he couldn't believe it. The prices people were willing to pay for good work almost made his eyes fall out of his head. He was able to charge thousands of pounds to do something he loved and was good at.

For someone who had lived his entire life in poverty, he couldn't believe his turn of luck. It had taken many years, but eventually he'd even been able to get a mortgage and buy a place of his own, something he'd never had before.

He kept both his home and workshop in low light. Sunlight wasn't good for his work, bleaching their fur and spoiling their skin. He kept curtains closed and blinds pulled down. It meant that he lived in the near dark, and that any neighbours, as distant as they were, whispered about him being the strange man who collected dead things.

He didn't mind. It meant people left him be, and that was just how he liked it. He'd learned a long time ago that people couldn't be trusted. Even the ones you thought you could trust used and manipulated and twisted things around to fit what they wanted.

Bryce had always been careful to research anyone who got in contact with him to do a job. He was fully aware that his craft attracted what many people would consider weirdos. In fact, he was most likely thought of as one of those weirdos himself.

Perhaps he was.

For the most part, the people who touched base with him did so for genuine reasons. He was mostly cautious of the ones who contacted him because they wanted a beloved pet to be immortalised. They often did so in the heat of the moment, when grief clutched at their souls, and they never imagined being able to part with their beloved friend. That time was not the right one to make such a decision.

Time tended to be a far greater healer than having a beloved pet immortalised in one position. Those people tended to be time-wasters and, once those initial claws of grief had released their hold, they changed their minds.

It was those pets he now had sitting on his surfaces or hung up on the walls. Of course, he told the client that the pet had been sent off for cremation, but that was never true. How would they know the small vial of ashes that was returned to them was a combination of so many other pets that had been cremated together, and didn't include any ashes of their precious animal?

Things had been going well for him up until the day Gary Carter had got in touch and told Bryce of his grief for his dead dog.

The moment he'd heard the name Gary Carter, it had been like someone had smashed him around the skull with a sledgehammer. His heart had thundered, and his mouth had run dry. He'd told himself it couldn't possibly be the same man, but with a name and address, it was easy to do a search to find out whatever he needed to know.

Sure enough, it was him.

Almost thirty years had passed. No wonder he hadn't recognised the voice. The past he had worked so hard to forget—no, not just forget, he had tried to eradicate it, to kill it, to become someone else—was suddenly back in his present.

Memories had pummelled him like stormy waves on a cliff face. He'd wanted to beat at the sides of his head with his fists and try to drive them out again, but it was no good. The floodgates had opened, and he couldn't figure out how to shut them again.

All the anger and humiliation he'd experienced as Philip Ross returned to him with full force.

He'd turned Gary Carter's name over and over in his head, repeating it as a mantra. But that wasn't the only name. Now his memories were returning, other names had come with it. Others who'd betrayed him. How could he live like this, knowing they were out there, living all these years with that secret buried inside them? Did they even think about what they'd done? Did they give him any thought at all? Most likely not.

He might have killed off Philip Ross, but he'd also brought him back again.

If the people from back then had wanted to keep his secret so badly, he'd make sure they could also take it to the grave.

Chapter Thirty-Five

Ryan and Mallory arrived at Bryce Ogden's property just as several response vehicles pulled up. Ryan had also made sure they had an ambulance on standby. He didn't know if they would find any other victims in the property, but, if there were, they may need immediate medical assistance.

They'd deliberately cut all sirens on the approach so as not to give Ogden—or was it Philip Ross, he didn't know how to think of him—a warning that they were coming. They were surrounded by countryside here, and it would be too easy for the perpetrator to slip out the back and vanish into one of the fields. Of course, that was assuming the suspect was even home. He might not be, though, with the fact that he worked here, as well as lived, it was a good place to start.

The property was located on the outskirts of Bristol, not far from where Gary Carter's car had been found. It stood alone on a country lane, a small gravel driveway leading up to the house. There were a couple of outbuildings as well, and a garden that looked like it hadn't been maintained in a very long time.

"No one would hear the victims screaming out here," Ryan commented, climbing out of the car.

Mallory's lips thinned. "It's pretty remote."

Ryan motioned for the team to gather in so he could ensure everyone knew what was expected of them.

As he spoke, he noticed Mallory standing straight, her neck craned.

"What is it, Sergeant?" he asked.

"We need to get in there. I'm pretty sure that's Olwen Morgan's car parked just out of view."

He followed her line of sight and caught a glimpse of mustard yellow between the bushes.

"Shit, you're right."

The car had been parked behind an overgrown hedge, out of sight of the main road.

He needed to consider the possibility that Olwen Morgan was there willingly, perhaps working with Bryce. But there was more of a chance she'd become another victim. The way the vehicle was positioned reminded him of Gary Carter's car—someone was trying to hide it.

"We need to move, everyone," he told the rest of the team. "Someone's life is in immediate danger."

Ryan signalled for officers to go around the back of the property, blocking the perpetrator's escape routes. If he was in that house, they would get him. He just hoped they weren't too late to save Olwen's life.

He deeply regretted not putting an officer on to watch over Olwen. He'd known that she may be in danger. Yes, he may have advised her to stay with someone else, but that clearly hadn't been enough. The killer had tracked her down anyway.

He let the uniformed officers lead the way. One tried the door, hammered on it, but when there was no response, he didn't hesitate to donkey-kick the door in. It flew inwards, and the police stormed the building.

Ryan and Mallory followed them in.

Shouts of 'police' and 'clear' filled the property as the place was searched room by room.

"There's no one here," one of the uniformed officers announced.

Ryan put his hands on his hips. "We're missing something."

"What about the outbuildings?" Mallory suggested.

"Damn it."

They should have searched those at the same time, though he didn't have enough people for that. He just hoped that the commotion hadn't warned Philip/Bryce that they were coming, and so forced his hand. At least they had the property surrounded, so Ryan would have known if the man had tried to make a run for it.

They exited the building and stepped back out into the bright autumn sunshine. Ryan quickly scanned the outsides of the outbuildings. A couple were just flimsy wooden sheds—not strong enough to keep anyone contained—but the third was a newer metal structure. A closer look revealed padlocks on the windows and an open lock on the door. What was being kept inside that would need such security?

The police officers surrounded the building. One positioned himself at the door, preparing to kick it open, but it was already unlocked. Just as they'd done at the house, they entered with shouts of 'police'.

Ryan and Mallory followed.

The inside of the building had been done up like the interior of a house. Plastered walls and ceilings, a carpeted floor. It was full of furniture, too—old-fashioned dark wood. But that wasn't what caught Ryan's attention the most. From every wall and surface, eyes of glass stared down at him. Larger animal heads mounted on the walls, birds forever perched on pieces of wood made to look like tree stumps, fish attached to frames.

"Officer with a Taser," an officer shouted from an adjoining room. "Drop the weapon right now."

Ryan and Mallory exchanged a glance and hurried through.

Olwen Morgan was on the floor. Philip/Bryce stood over her, a scalpel in his hand. They both had their heads turned in the direction of the police as they made their entrance.

One of the uniformed officers had his Taser aimed at the man who'd once been known as Philip Ross.

Philip/Bryce froze, but instead of dropping the blade, his fingers tightened around the handle, his knuckles showing white.

"I said drop the weapon!" the officer commanded.

With a scream of rage and terror, Olwen launched herself off the floor.

"Olwen, no!" Ryan just managed to shout, but it was too late.

Olwen caught Philip off-guard—his attention focused purely on the police—and collided with his legs with her full body weight. He fell back, his heel catching on one of the fallen statues, and he landed straight onto one of the animal heads mounted on his wall. Ryan winced at the sound of flesh puncturing. The man who had once been known as Philip Ross let out a scream of agony. He tried to pull himself off the boar's tusks, but both shoulders had been impaled.

"Jesus Christ," Ryan muttered then called over his shoulder, "we need paramedics in here, now!"

He doubted the man's injuries would be life-threatening, but at least he wouldn't have to cuff him just yet.

Philip—Bryce—wasn't going anywhere.

Ryan placed himself directly in front of the man. "Bryce Ogden, you are under arrest for the abduction and murders of Gary Carter, Jillian Griffiths, and Victoria Fletcher, and for the abduction of Olwen Morgan. You do not have to say anything, but it may harm your defence if you do not mention when questioned something which you later rely on in court. Anything you do say may be given in evidence."

Ryan made way for the paramedics. He imagined they'd first have to get the boar head off the wall, and then transport the prisoner to hospital with the boar head still impaled until they could get him into surgery.

He didn't like that it meant this murdering son of a bitch would get some cushy time on a hospital ward instead of in a cell where he belonged, but he also wanted Philip/Bryce to remain alive for a good long time so he could serve several life terms in jail as his punishment.

A second set of paramedics attended to Olwen. She'd most likely been drugged—if past cases were anything to go by—though by the way she'd moved, he assumed those drugs had worn off. She might be injured in other ways, however, and needed to be checked over. The psychological harm would probably be the thing that she'd need the most recovery from.

Chapter Thirty-Six

"Have you got everything?" Mallory asked Oliver as they made one final trip back to the car to unload.

This was supposed to be just a trial run of Oliver staying at the house, but he'd insisted on bringing almost everything from his bedroom. It had resulted in the car being full to the roof, and bags and other items stacked on top of the seats and in the footwells. They'd emptied out most of it now, with the help of the others living at the home, and some of the staff as well.

"I think so," Oliver said.

Mallory leaned back into the car. "Oh, what about your kettle bell? It's still on the floor of the passenger seat."

Oliver wrinkled his nose. "No, I don't need that."

She wished he'd mentioned that before she'd lugged the bloody thing all the way down from his bedroom. It wasn't as though she'd ever even seen him use it recently. It had just been one of those random things he'd suddenly insisted he needed and used every day for about a week before never touching it again.

"Okay, as long as you're sure."

She took in the house that was now going to be Oliver's home, and a painful lump caught in her throat. She couldn't believe he was actually moving out.

A shout came from the front door. "Come on, Ollie! I'm waiting for you."

It was Paul, Oliver's new housemate.

Mallory forced a smile. "Looks like you're wanted."

Oliver glanced over his shoulder and nodded. "Yes. I have to go now."

Mallory opened her arms to him, and he fell into her, wrapping his arms around her waist and giving her one of those bear hugs she'd always loved so much. The tightness in her throat increased, and her nostrils flared as she battled against tears. She didn't want him to see her crying and feel bad about his choices.

Mallory forced herself to release him, blinking back tears.

"Now, remember that Mum and Dad will be over tomorrow to—"

But Oliver had already turned and was running up the steps leading to the front door, to where his friend was waiting.

She let out a sigh and turned back to her car. By the time she'd got behind the wheel, Oliver had already vanished inside the house.

She guessed it was time to go home as well.

On the drive back to her house, her emotions warred with each other, a combination of being weirdly sad but light at the same time. The world suddenly opened up to her. The sense of responsibility she'd felt for as long as she could remember lifted. Even when she'd been a teenager, she'd always taken care of Oliver. He was never a burden to her—she loved him and didn't think of him that way—but that he now wanted to live an independent life was something she needed to embrace.

Mallory stopped at a junction, the traffic lights showing red. It flicked back to green again, and she put the car into first gear and accelerated.

Sudden movement swerved into her right-side vision, followed by the crunch of metal and the screech of tyres on tarmac.

Mallory slammed forward and to the side, the airbag exploding, hitting her in the face. Her ears rang, and she tasted blood. The sweet chemical scent of the airbag—similar to that of cannabis smoke—filled her nostrils. What the hell just happened? The world seemed to turn in a slow circle around her.

A car had hit her.

On the passenger side, the door opened. Her vision was blurry. Someone must have witnessed the accident and come to help. How badly hurt was she? She tried to assess her injuries. She didn't think she was too hurt. Her head and neck ached and would probably feel a hundred times worse by tomorrow, but she didn't think there were any broken bones. It was more the shock than anything else.

A blurry hand reached for her, and the face beyond it took shape.

Mallory screamed.

It was Daniel. His nose was bloodied, and what had happened sank in. He'd deliberately hit her with his car.

"Come here, bitch."

He grabbed her arm and dragged her out of her seat. Her shoulder joint screeched with pain. She struggled and fought, but it was no good. He was far stronger than her.

"Get the fuck off me," she shrieked.

He continued to pull her. Soon she would be out of the car and onto the road, and what would he do then? There must be other people around who were witnessing what was happening. It was late afternoon and still daylight. Why was no one helping her?

In desperation, she scrabbled around, trying to find something to hold on to. Deep down, she knew that if he managed to get her out of the car, he would kill her. Her fingers closed around a metal handle, and she hung on to it. But instead of being something solid to keep her inside the vehicle, it moved as well. She realised what it was. Oliver's kettle bell weight.

Mallory lifted it up and swung her arm, wide and fast.

It connected with the side of Daniel's head. The crack was impossibly loud, and he slumped. His fingers released their painful hold on her, and he collapsed to the ground.

People had pulled up behind the two crashed vehicles. She heard someone shout to call an ambulance. The police would be here soon, too.

Mallory got out of the car and staggered to her feet but only managed a couple of steps before she crumpled again. She'd only wanted to put distance between her and Daniel. She didn't want to be anywhere near him, whether he was alive or dead.

Dead? Could he really be dead? Did that make her a murderer? Was she really going to go to prison for that son of a bitch? There were witnesses, though. She was aware of people and vehicles all around her. They'd have seen Daniel deliberately driving into her car and then trying to drag her out. But what if they thought he was trying to help her by dragging her out of the vehicle and she just attacked him? It would make her look like the bad guy again, even though no one knew the background to the story.

Someone crouched beside her and touched her shoulder. She let out a cry of shock and flinched away.

"Sorry, sorry," the person—a woman—said. "I just wanted to make sure you're all right."

All right? No, she wasn't all right. She wasn't sure she'd ever be now.

"Is—" Mallory managed to say, though her voice sounded distant and not like her own. "Is he dead?"

The woman glanced over her shoulder. "I'm not sure, but he deliberately ran through that red light and drove into the side of you."

Mallory closed her eyes. "He's my ex. He's been stalking me."

"Oh my God. I'm so sorry."

Sirens cut through the air.

"The police are coming," the woman said. "We'll tell them everything. It'll be fine."

Mallory wasn't so sure about that. She didn't bother telling the woman that she was also with the police, and that one thing she'd learned over the past few months was that the police couldn't always save you.

Chapter Thirty-Seven

Olwen took a breath and pushed through the door.

They'd agreed to meet somewhere different this time –not the old pub where they used to hang out as teenagers. This place had the modern décor of a gastropub, with the price list to match, but it was different enough that they felt like they were moving forwards instead of looking back.

These past few weeks had been the hardest of Olwen's life. Coming to terms with who her mother had been was both painful yet cathartic.

It had all made sense to her once she'd learned the truth.

Now she understood why her childhood had been so strange, why she's never really felt loved, and why she'd been excluded from her parents' relationship. It had never been anything to do with who Olwen was as a person. Her mum and dad had shared a terrible, twisted secret—one that had ultimately created a monster in the form of Philip Ross—and that hadn't been Olwen's fault.

No matter how much she tried, she couldn't shift the shame at not only having blocked the incident with Philip and her mother from her memory, but also that her mother had been a child abuser and her father had done nothing to stop it.

It was unlikely her father would ever go to trial for his involvement. Not only would he not live long enough, but he also didn't have the mental capacity to do so. Olwen believed he remembered some of what happened back then—he wouldn't have had such a violent reaction when she'd had tried to talk to him that time, if he didn't—but the police were never going to get any information out of him.

Olwen had told the police she'd found Samuel Cole in her father's room shortly before she'd been taken, but the police investigation hadn't uncovered any involvement of Sam, or the others, with Philip. This, at least, had been a relief for her. The possibility they'd all been in on some conspiracy to have her murdered had kept her awake at night.

A few days ago, Andy had got back in touch and asked her to meet them again. She'd been very tempted to say no, then she'd given herself a kick up the backside. She still had questions she needed answers to, and she'd made a promise to herself that she'd ask them directly this time.

They were all waiting for her in the gastropub—Andy, Tina, and Sam. It was a terrible and horrifying thing that bound them now, but they were also the only people who really understood. The atmosphere was sombre, but it was also compassionate.

"I'd considered not coming," she admitted as she approached the table.

Andy frowned. "Why?"

"Isn't that obvious? It makes me feel sick just thinking about it."

"We feel just as bad," Tina said. "None of us did or said anything to help either."

Andy pursed his lips and twisted his pint glass in his hands. "We used to joke about it. Teasing Philip about how Elanor liked him. Even when Philip clearly didn't think it was funny, we didn't stop."

"You knew then?" Olwen asked. "You knew for certain?"

He shook his head. No, but we knew something was going on. That she paid him too much attention, and things got really uncomfortable at times. We should have stood up for him when he finally tried to tell people. If we had, it might have made all the difference."

"People's lives could have been saved," Samuel said.

Olwen blinked back tears. "I feel responsible. They were—are—my parents."

Andy reached across the table and took her hand. "You can't choose who you're born to, Olwen. Look at us. None of our parents wanted us, or were too drug-addled or booze-soaked to be able to take care of us. I remember when I was around ten, I'd done something to upset my mum and she locked me in the garden shed all night as punishment. But that was on her. It wasn't my fault, and you need to think of what your parents did the same way. It wasn't your fault either."

Olwen blinked back tears and sniffed. "Deep down, I know that. I think it's just going to take a little time for my head and heart to catch up."

"We understand," Andy said, looking around at the others. "Don't we?"

They all nodded.

Olwen thought of something. "I have to ask a question." She directed her focus on one of them in particular. "Why were you in my dad's room that day, Sam? You know I thought you were the one who'd kidnapped me from my car. I never expected Philip to walk into that horrible room with all the taxidermy statues. I thought it was going to be you."

He twisted his lips and shook his head. "I'm sorry. I guess I wanted closure as well. Even though we didn't know the full extent of what your mum and dad had been doing, they still weren't nice to us. I wanted to see him as the man he'd become and not the one I'd carried around in my head all these years. I couldn't face up to your mother, because she was dead, so he was the next best thing. I wanted to reassure myself that he couldn't hurt anyone anymore."

Olwen accepted his explanation. "I understand that. I won't be visiting him again. It hurts, but I just can't. I can't look at him without thinking about how he stood by and allowed Mum to do what she did. If he'd stepped in, things would have been different."

Tina caught her eye across the table. "He doesn't have long left, Olwen. Aren't you worried you'll regret it if you don't go?"

"Maybe I will, but I just can't do it."

"You have other family, don't you?" Tina asked.

Olwen had talked to her aunt a lot over the past few weeks, long conversations that involved plenty of tears and wine, and run late into the night.

Aunt Milly had been understandably shocked by the news. At first, she'd wanted to disbelieve it—like so many had when Philip tried to tell them his story—but in the end she'd had no choice but to accept the truth. Milly had always painted Olwen's dad as being the bad one, the one who'd corrupted her much younger, impressionable sister, but it hadn't been like that at all. They'd both been bad people, and maybe had recognised that in each other. Like Olwen, Millicent had to reshape the memory she'd had of her sister. It was a kind of grief, especially when that person was already gone.

She couldn't help but ask her aunt why her parents had even bothered having her. Had she been an accident? Milly hadn't been able to look her in the eye then, but she'd replied, "I think your mother had always hoped for a boy."

Olwen didn't even want to process exactly what that meant.

Though it was hard for them both, Olwen also came away feeling as though she was closer to her aunt than she had ever been. Maybe, in some way, her mum had always been between them, but now that obstacle to their relationship had been shifted.

"Yes, I do," she said.

"And she has us, too," Andy insisted.

Olwen found herself smiling at him in gratitude.

One thing Olwen did know, despite everything that had happened, she no longer felt so alone.

Chapter Thirty-Eight

Ryan was down a detective sergeant, and the office simply didn't feel the same without Mallory in it. She was taking some time out—partly enforced after what had happened—while investigations were being carried out. Now that Daniel no longer posed a threat to her, she was happy to stay home.

Daniel Williamson hadn't died from the blow to the head, but it was likely he wouldn't be the same man any more. He'd suffered a bleed on the brain, though he'd also hit his head when he'd driven his car directly into Mallory's, so the defence was arguing that the bleed could have originated from his own doing.

Meanwhile, Ryan was busy putting the final pieces together on the case.

Olwen Morgan was having to come to terms with the fact her parents had abused teenage boys while she'd been growing up, but physically, she'd been left unharmed by the incident.

A separate investigation had been opened up into how something like that had happened back in the nineties. There was no doubt that there had been a cover-up, and questions would be asked about who was involved and what procedures hadn't been followed. The damage it had caused Philip Ross was immeasurable, though he'd managed to put it behind him. He'd put his own obituary in the paper and changed his name.

He'd wanted Philip Ross to be dead. He had been let down by so many people. He couldn't carry it with him his whole life, so the only way he could think of continuing to live was to let the boy he'd once been die.

It had worked until Gary Carter had come back into his life.

That moment seemed to have triggered something inside Philip. It brought back his fury from those days when he'd been a teenager. It had taken him back to that time when he'd been a vulnerable teenage boy, and he'd set upon his mission to punish everyone he'd blamed for letting him down all those years ago.

A murmur of interest rose around the office, and Ryan took his attention from the case to glance up.

Mallory had entered the office. She was dressed casually in skinny black jeans, boots, and a t-shirt with a band name across it that Ryan had never heard of. She still had the ghost of the car crash across her face in bruises and grazes, but they were healing. Even with everything that had happened, she looked more relaxed than he'd seen her in some time.

Everyone greeted her warmly, clapping her on the back, shaking her hand, or pulling her into a hug.

Ryan got to his feet as well, and she caught his eye and smiled, then headed over.

"Welcome back, stranger."

"Thanks. I'm not back for work, though."

"No?" He hadn't really been expecting her to be.

"I just heard," Mallory said. "I won't be charged for what happened with Daniel. There are too many witnesses that describe him driving into me deliberately and then dragging me from the car. It was clearly self-defence, especially considering he has a restraining order on him. He'll be the one spending time in prison once he's out of hospital."

"Best place for him. I don't think he's going to be causing you any more problems."

"No, I guess not."

She paused and twisted her hands in front of her body. There was clearly something she wanted to tell him.

"What is it?" he asked.

"When I am cleared to be able to come back to work, I think I'm going to ask for a transfer."

She'd surprised him. "You are? I thought you liked this team."

"I do, and I'm going to miss everyone, but I need a change of scenery."

He understood. "You'll be missed."

"I won't go far, and I'll stay in touch. I need to be close by enough to be able to still see Ollie every week. But he doesn't need me as much as he once did, and the house feels too big for me to rattle around in on my own." She gave her head a slight shake. "Honestly, I just don't like being there anymore. There are so many memories, and though lots are good, the bad ones overwhelm them."

"Is Oliver going to be okay with you moving away?"

She gave a small, one-shouldered shrug. "He moved away first, and that's a good thing. I'll come up and see him every day I have off, and he still has our parents. He can come down and see me, too."

"You think you know where you'd like to move to, then?"

She nodded. "Yes, there's a sergeant's job opened up down in Exeter. It's an hour on the train, so not far at all, but far enough for me to get a fresh start."

"First Craig, and now you...the team won't feel like the team anymore."

"What about you?" she asked. "Are you going to be all right?"

"Yeah, I think so. Donna has sold the house, too, for similar reasons to yours. Lots of good memories, but too many bad ones to be able to move forward."

"And you and Donna are all right?"

"Yeah, we're starting afresh, too. It's not as though we'll ever forget Hayley, but we're learning how to live with her loss, together."

THAT EVENING, RYAN sat with Donna on the sofa in their old house.

"I found somewhere," she told him. "I think you'll like it."

His stomach twisted. He still hated the idea of selling the house—what had been their home. The whole place was filled with memories of their daughter, and it felt like Donna was trying to forget her.

"Are you sure you want to do this?" he checked.

"I'm sure," she said. "I don't want to feel like I've been punched with pain and grief every time I walk into a room. Do you know how hard it is to walk past her bedroom door every day and know our daughter will never be in there? I still have moments where I think I hear her, and my heart lifts, but then I remember that she's gone, and it all comes crashing back down on me. The memory and trauma of when we first lost her hasn't gone away. It's like it's buried deep inside me, just waiting for that flicker of a memory or a thought to bring it all rushing back again. I can't keep living like that. It's not healthy. We need to move on." She handed him her iPad with the details of the house. "Just take a look."

He caught sight of the address. "That's down the road from my place."

She smiled. "I know. That's why I thought you'd like it."

The house was a new-build, with a driveway and three bedrooms, and a tidy back garden. It was much the same as many of the other new-build properties in the area, but if she liked it, then he would support her.

"It looks great," he said. "But you realise if you're just down the road from me, I'll be popping in all the time."

She threw him a flirtatious smile. "Why do you think I like it?"

He slipped his arm around her waist and kissed her hard on the mouth. "In which case, I love it. How long do you think it'll take for the sale to go through?"

"Not long. There's no chain, so there's no reason it won't go through in the next couple of months."

"I'm happy for you, Donna. Really, I am."

She narrowed her eyes at him quizzically. "You sure about that?"

"I'm not going to pretend I won't miss the old house, and that it'll feel strange knowing another family is living there, but you deserve to get what you want. You've had a hard run of things. I want you to be happy."

Once upon a time, he hadn't believed that he'd truly meant that. But lately, the anger and resentment that had been residing inside him for so long had melted away and taken many of his other issues with it. His OCD no longer plagued him as it once had, and the intrusive thoughts had vanished. He wasn't sure he'd ever be someone who could live a calm and peaceful life—especially not with his job—but he was definitely closer to that goal.

He could be happy, too.

Acknowledgements

When I started this book, I realised I have absolutely no knowledge about trains or what happens when someone—or something—is on the track. A mutual friend put me in touch with Martyn Trathen, who works on the trains, and who kindly answered my many questions. Anything I got wrong is purely down to me needing to make some tweaks to fit the story and not Martyn's information.

I always feel like I'm thanking the same people in my books, but the fact is that I have a wonderful group of editors and proofreaders who I always rely on. So thanks to Emmy Ellis, Jessica Fraser, Tammy Payne and Jacqueline Beard for making sure my books are fit for readers' eyes before they go to publication!

Finally, thanks to you, the reader, for following Ryan and Mallory's journey through this series. I'm sorry if you're disappointed it's come to an end, but keep an eye out for an announcement about a possible Christmas special!

Until next time,
MK

About the Author

M K Farrar had penned more than twenty novels of psychological noir and crime fiction. A British author, she lives in the countryside with her three children and a menagerie of rescue pets.

When she's not writing—which isn't often—she balances out all the murder with baking and binge-watching shows on Netflix.

You can find out more about M K and grab a free book via her website, https://mkfarrar.com

She can also be emailed at mk@mkfarrar.com. She loves to hear from readers!

Also by the Author

DI Erica Swift Thriller
The Eye Thief
The Silent One
The Artisan
The Child Catcher
The Body Dealer
The Mimic
The Gathering Man
The Only Witness
The Foundling

Crime after Crime series, written with M A Comley
Watching Over Me
Down to Sleep
If I Should Die

Standalone Psychological Thrillers
Some They Lie
On His Grave
Down to Sleep
21 Days

Printed in Great Britain
by Amazon